Y0-CRG-034

DATE DUE

AN AVALON ROMANCE

SECONDHAND DREAMS
Nancy Morgan

Roseanna MacAuly dreamed about owning a fashionable clothing boutique. She dreamed about it every time she was teased at school for wearing her sister's patched hand-me-down dresses. She dreamed about it every time her thrift store shoes pinched.

But that dream gets put on hold when she inherits a run-down secondhand shop. How strange life can seem sometimes. Why would fate have chosen to give her the one kind of store she didn't want?

And it's not just old clothes that Roseanna wants out of her life. Her distaste for anything used extends to men. After a disastrous relationship with a divorced man, she vows to stay far away from men who have been married. So when handsome, bedeviling, and divorced Simon Oakes opens his antique shop across the street, Roseanna is faced with a new problem. What is she going to do about her secondhand man?

SECONDHAND DREAMS

•

Nancy Morgan

AVALON BOOKS
NEW YORK

Published by Thomas Bouregy & Co., Inc.
160 Madison Avenue, New York, NY 10016

PRINTED IN THE UNITED STATES OF AMERICA
ON ACID-FREE PAPER
BY HADDON CRAFTSMEN, BLOOMSBURG, PENNSYLVANIA

To my devoted husband, Jeff, and superior son, Cody.

Chapter One

"Let me know if I can answer any questions," Roseanna MacAuly said, beaming at her first customer of the day. "There are a lot of treasures here."

"I hope I'll find one," replied the plump, middle-aged woman who was eagerly sorting through a display of vintage kitchenware. "I just adore these secondhand shops." She ran her finger around the rim of a large ceramic bowl, checking for chips, then tucked it under her arm. With a satisfied smile she said, "You never know what might turn up. When I saw all the things outside and your grand-opening sign, I just had to stop."

"Help yourself to cookies and coffee," Roseanna offered, gesturing to the refreshment stand she had just set up. A delicious aroma scented the air. The coffee was doing its job, covering the stale odor she had not

1

quite been able to eliminate, even with liberal usage of pine cleaners and lemon polish.

Leaving the woman to shop on her own, Roseanna propped open the double glass doors, then picked up an antique wedding gown to take outside. As she stepped onto the broad front porch, its wood aged to a silvery gray, she paused to admire the scene before her.

Between the store and the three blooming dogwood trees that lined the street was a spacious courtyard, its uneven bricks worn to a soft pink and edged with green moss. Today, the area overflowed with chests and dressers and tables, plus a huge assortment of other goods, all her best merchandise. Illuminated by the April morning sunlight, it looked wonderful.

A feeling of pride welled within Roseanna, not for the old, often tattered wares she had displayed with such painstaking care, but for the months of hard work that had led up to this moment. A secondhand store was not her dream, but since fate had been so kind as to place one in her hands, she intended to make the best of it.

Movement caught her eye. A tall, dark-haired man was jogging across the street toward her. She had only just opened, and had another customer already!

She went to hang the wedding gown on a mannequin beside a Victorian dresser. In the dresser's tall oval mirror she caught sight of herself and the shimmering garment reflected in the glass. Even though it was used, the glorious dress took her breath away. Letting impulse overcome her, she drew the gown close until it hid her blue skirt and sweater outfit.

Long, wavy auburn hair bunched over her shoulders to frame her face. The combination of excitement and cool morning air had infused her cheeks with a rosy hue.

The sound of footsteps snagged Roseanna's attention. The dark-haired man was heading in her direction. He stopped a few feet away to examine a rolltop desk, and she watched in the mirror as he opened a drawer to peer inside. Sunlight accentuated the strong lines of his handsome face, and the breeze ruffled his thick brown hair like invisible fingers. He ran his hand along the oak as though he were stroking a living creature. Observing, Roseanna could not help noticing the breadth of his shoulders and the muscular, tanned arms that were revealed by the rolled sleeves of his crisp white shirt. The impression of masculine vitality and easy confidence was stamped on her mind. Her gaze wandered up and collided with his, reflected back to her. Caught staring, and keenly aware of the way she clutched the dress to herself, Roseanna felt her cheeks flush.

His eyes twinkled. "You will make a beautiful blushing bride."

Tongue-tied from embarrassment, Roseanna felt her face grow even hotter, if that were possible. Stepping away from the mirror, she quickly slipped the dress onto the mannequin and began to button the front. A covert glance over her shoulder found his attention had shifted to her new sign. She'd had it mounted just the day before on the turn-of-the-century, two-story wood building that housed both her shop and upstairs apartment. She had told the artist—the only one she could afford being her part-time employee, Tim—that she needed something that would grab people's attention. Her store was located at the outer edge of Annapolis, Maryland, and her neighbors, a catering business and a sailmaker, were not exactly huge draws. Lacking foot traffic, she needed something to entice people off the busy street. Tim had done his utmost to fulfill her request.

In brilliant gold letters, the name *Treasures* arched across the top of the sign, and at the bottom a chest overflowed with sparkling jewels and gleaming doubloons. Smack in the middle knelt a pirate who bore a wicked resemblance to Roseanna.

Tim had painted the pirate life-size, with her red hair billowing like a tanbark sail in a nor'easter. She was decked out in a full black skirt bunched up to expose bare calves and feet, and a low-cut white ruffled blouse with a gold medallion dangling at her throat. And as a final touch, Tim had given her a mischievous grin, as though the lady pirate had downed a bit too much cutthroat rum and was looking for trouble.

As the attractive man studied her portrait, Roseanna felt an impish spark of delight at having been made to look so bold and alluring. Glancing over her shoulder, she met his gaze once again. A corner of his mouth hitched upward as he treated her to a broad wink.

When an arm slipped around her waist just then, Roseanna nearly catapulted out of her skin.

"Getting married?" asked her friend Karyn, having appeared out of nowhere.

Roseanna looked around. The man was gone.

"I was just going to work. I thought I'd stop and wish you luck on your big day." Karyn squeezed Roseanna's hand. "You're going to do great."

Karyn knew how important the success of the sale was to Roseanna. They had become friends on Roseanna's first day as owner of Treasures. Karyn loved funky old clothes and had begged to check out the shop before Roseanna opened to the public. Since she worked at Crab Claw Catering next door, Roseanna saw her often.

Dressed today in one of her favorite retro clothing outfits—black pedal pushers, a pink-and-black sweater, and sparkling rhinestone earrings—Karyn looked stunning.

"Let me see that," Karyn said, arching back to eye the wedding dress. "Check out this beadwork. Wow! It would cost a fortune to buy this today. I'd save it for myself if I were you."

Roseanna fluffed its satin skirt for full effect. "Are you serious? A used wedding dress?"

"Vintage," Karyn corrected. "One of a kind."

Roseanna wrinkled her nose in distaste. "It is lovely, but I could never wear it. It belonged to someone else. I'd feel the same about wearing this secondhand dress as I would marrying a secondhand husband."

Karyn looked in the mirror and smoothed her sleek pageboy haircut. "I suppose your future mate will have lived his entire life ignoring women . . . that is, until he sets his adoring eyes on you. And his sweet lips will have never before been kissed." She formed her fuchsia mouth into a pucker and made a loud smacking noise.

Roseanna rolled her eyes at her friend's teasing antics. "Kissed, somewhat, is okay. Previous girlfriends, I guess that's inevitable. But divorced—" She shook her head stubbornly, sending her long red hair flying. "Been there, done that. I learned my lesson. I'm not going to try patching up any more broken hearts."

"Miss?" A voice rang out.

Roseanna turned to see the plump woman she had spoken to earlier and left Karyn to assist her customer. Other people had arrived and were milling through the courtyard, creating a busy, festive atmosphere.

"How can I assist you?" Roseanna asked as she hurried over.

Under one arm, the woman still clutched the bowl, which was now filled with various items. "Is this table real cherrywood?"

"It certainly is. And it's in fine condition," Roseanna assured her, putting lots of enthusiasm and salesmanship into her pitch. "The small scars and dents add character you can't buy in new furniture."

Out of the corner of her eye, she caught sight of the man again. Her heartbeat quickened, and she craned to get a better view. He was crouched, intent on the battered seaman's chest she had placed beneath one of the dogwoods. She kept a discreet eye on him as he pushed himself up to his full height, braced his hands on lean hips, and surveyed the area. When he turned in her direction Roseanna ducked her head, lest he catch her ogling him.

"Character?" Her customer repeated with a merry laugh, jerking Roseanna's attention back. "I dare say this piece has enough character to star on its own late-night talk show."

"Quite desirable in an antique," Roseanna countered.

"What a fantastic piece," Karyn cooed, as she joined them. "It has all six original chairs, I see. And a wing, too. How perfect."

"How sturdy is it?" Although she addressed Roseanna, the woman kept a watchful eye on Karyn.

Roseanna realized her customer had gotten the idea Karyn was in competition to buy the table. She silently motioned for her friend to get lost, but when the woman stooped to check the underside of the table, Karyn just drew a huge dollar sign in the air.

"Don't you have to go to work?" Roseanna whispered urgently. She glimpsed the man nearby. With any luck neither he, nor anyone else, had seen Karyn's sign language.

"Who owned this table before?" asked the woman from below.

"It originally belonged to a celebrated Capitol Hill hostess," Roseanna repeated the story she had been told. "She was renowned for her sparkling personality and her interest in séances. She—"

"Oh, dear," the woman exclaimed as she straightened, with some effort, by bracing a hand on the tabletop. "There is a problem. I'm afraid there's a wobble. A definite wobble." To prove her point, she pressed down on the table several more times. It thumped heartily against the bricks.

"Yes, I know. You see, the prior owner says this shorter leg had great significance," Roseanna contin-

ued, undaunted. "The hostess had it cut off for a reason."

"You don't say," the woman murmured.

"At one time, a delicate situation arose in which she
couldn't avoid inviting a particularly long-winded
politician to a small, intimate dinner party."

By the intrigued look on her customer's face Roseanna knew she had her hooked. But when the dark-
haired man walked by, his brows arched mockingly
and his mouth curled in an incredulous expression, her
excitement waned.

"Whenever the guest launched into a lengthy ti-
rade," she went on, "the hostess would secretly rock
the table and create a mysterious and hilarious diver-
sion."

Karyn clapped her hands in delight. "How extraor-
dinary. I'll bet she used it after that for table-tipping
séances." She proceeded to gaze at the piece of furniture as though she might expire on the spot if she
could not have it for her very own. "And what modest
amount are you asking for this treasure?"

"One moment," the woman interjected, grappling
for her pocketbook. "I believe I was here first."

With a dramatic sigh, Karyn shook her head, causing her rhinestone earrings to twinkle in the sunlight.
"Oh, dear me. So you were. I guess I'll have to find
my own treasure another day, for now I'm off to
work."

Roseanna led her customer inside for payment. After making arrangements for delivery the woman left,
and Roseanna came outside on the porch feeling exhilarated from her first sale. Birds chirped in the trees

and cars sped past on the busy road. Some of the people who had been milling around earlier had gone inside and some had left, leaving only one person in the courtyard.

At the sight of the tall man her heart began beating a little faster. Because he faced away from her and seemed preoccupied with a wooden filing cabinet, she was able to approach unnoticed. She took her time, examining him as she went. As she came nearer she saw he towered over her by several inches; his broad shoulders were intimidating. She couldn't keep her gaze from roaming downward past a trim waist to powerful legs rooted firmly to the ground. He radiated strength and a kind of raw masculinity she found very unnerving.

Halting three feet away, she tucked her unruly locks behind her ears and smoothed her skirt. "May I help you?" she asked, grateful her voice sounded quite normal, in spite of herself.

When he turned to face her, eyes the color of aged oak bore into hers. At once she knew he possessed an intelligence as formidable as his physical prowess. Then he smiled a slow and easy smile that carved a dimple in his left cheek and completely disarmed her.

"Ah, yes, the blushing bride. Well, Ms.—" He paused in question.

"MacAuly. Roseanna MacAuly."

"I think you might be able assist me." He didn't sound terribly eager. "You are the proprietor of this store, I take it?"

"Yes, I am."

He nodded in a matter-of-fact way, as if he had

assumed that already. "I've noticed you here. You've been working hard on this place."

She thought he looked familiar, too, but couldn't place him. "I've been here since February, trying to get the store ready to open."

"I've shopped here several times before, but it's been at least a year. It had a different name, and I remember an elderly woman here then. She was a character! Full of spunk. Red hair, like yours, but it must have been dyed. She always managed to sell me something."

"That was Matilda MacAuly, my great-aunt." Rose-anna felt a prick of sadness at the loss of her beloved relative. "Aunt Tildy passed on this winter and left me the store. Today is the first day I've been open."

"I see. So you're brand new to this business." His steady gaze gave her the uneasy feeling he was assessing everything about her.

"Not exactly," she answered. Trying to ignore her discomfort, she went on to explain, "I used to work for my aunt during the summers when I was a teenager. I think I learned enough then to do a credible job now."

"Doesn't it take a great deal of knowledge to operate a store like this?" he asked casually.

She shrugged. "A great deal of elbow grease is more like it. My dear Aunt Tildy was an incredible pack rat and not much on cleaning. I had to tackle boxes stacked to the ceiling and remove enough dust to grow a garden. The hardest part of operating this business so far has been just getting ready to open the doors."

"How do you feel about your prices?"

"I think they're fair, if that's what you mean," she responded, a bit puzzled before deciding he only meant to begin haggling. "Of course," she hurried on, "I'm willing to consider reasonable offers."

She was familiar with this routine from her previous shop experience, back when Treasures had been named, with utter lack of charm, the Community Thrift Store. She recalled that as an awkward teenager she had been embarrassed to help out at the run-down shop and had felt resentful when customers asked for a price even lower than the pittance her great-aunt had wanted.

She glanced around now, mentally assessing her price tags. She had been rushed to get the store open and had mostly just guessed what people might pay for an item. In truth, she hadn't given the task much thought, but she had marked things as low as possible, in hopes of keeping her customers coming back.

"It looks to me like you have some bargains here," he continued. The slight breeze was playing with his hair again, making it catch the sunshine and show off its luster.

"That's right," she responded perkily. "And you never know when you'll find a treasure."

"The name you chose gives you a great line," he observed, not critically at all.

"I hope it's true also."

For a long moment he studied her, and she could have sworn she saw amusement flickering in his eyes. Then he got down to business. "I'm interested in several of your treasures. The rolltop desk and this filing cabinet. The ship model. The watchmaker's cabinet.

The red oriental rug. The rattan chair. A Montague Dawson print you have inside, and the Fiestaware." He paused, and sucked in a breath, as if debating. "And I suppose I'll go for that dresser in front of which you were modeling so charmingly."

Roseanna had to keep herself from gasping out loud. *The desk, the chair, the watchmaker's cabinet* . . . If he bought all the items he just mentioned, her weekend sale would be off to an incredible start.

"I believe you were asking—" His expression serious now, he lowered his gaze to the small notebook cupped in his palm and read off the amount. "Considering the quantity of my purchases, I'd like a discount."

Still astounded by his lengthy list, she had to pause for a calming breath before offering him ten percent off.

A slight tightening of his lips revealed his dissatisfaction with that suggestion. He crossed his muscled arms and turned his attention to her sign, which he stared at while coming to a decision. At long last he turned his bold gaze on her once more and said in a soft, deeply masculine tone, "That's not enough."

Roseanna's temples began to throb. It was a good deal and she suspected he darn well knew it, but her desire to make the sale tugged at her fiercely. She decided to try standing firm. "My prices are already very low."

He sighed. It was a long, drawn-out, regretful breath she knew was for her benefit. When he closed his notebook in a deliberate fashion and tucked it into the back pocket of his slacks it became clear to her that he was no novice at this game. He cocked a brow in her direction, indicating she had better think again or he would leave empty handed.

Roseanna chewed her lip as indecision tugged at her. She had hoped she had grown out of her youthful dislike for bargaining, but now realized she found it just as nerve-wracking as she had before. Why hadn't her aunt left her the fashionable clothing boutique she yearned to own, instead of this run-down secondhand shop? Immediately contrite for her ungratefulness, Roseanna whispered a swift, silent *Sorry* to the heavens.

Reminding herself to be thankful for his business, she adjusted her offer again, then copied his folded arms to let him know he had pushed her as far as she would go. When his features relaxed in a warming smile, complete with the boyish dimple, Roseanna realized she had succeeded.

Clasping his hand to seal the agreement, she felt a rush of excitement course through her veins. She blushed, became furious at the involuntary response—which only made it worse—then quickly blamed it on the thrill of making such a big sale.

"Do you deliver?" he asked, not giving any indication he noticed her distress. They headed into the store, where he produced a checkbook.

She handed him a pen. "For a fee."

"Yes, of course. That's what I expected. I can take some things myself right now. The heavier items I'd like brought over." He handed her the completed check.

She had to force herself not to stare at the dazzling figure he'd written in. "Where do you live?"

"They're not going to my home."

Roseanna cocked her head, wondering what he meant.

He withdrew his wallet and handed her a business card. Printed in flowing gold script was the name *Oakes Antiques,* flanked by the silhouettes of two oak trees.

He nodded at the elegant antique store across the street.

"I'm Simon Oakes. I recently bought that shop. You've just helped me add to my inventory."

Chapter Two

Understanding struck Roseanna like a slap on the face. She stood frozen to the spot, and when she realized she was gaping at him, closed her mouth with a snap.

An antiques dealer. No doubt he planned to take her merchandise to his store and offer it for sale at a much higher price than he had paid. Even though he had bargained with her fairly, the little-girl part of her felt cheated, bamboozled.

He turned toward the coffee stand. She had recently made a fresh pot and replenished her attractive assortment of cookies. "I'm starved. May I?" he asked politely.

Roseanna gritted her teeth. "Help yourself."

In seemingly complete composure he poured a cup and selected several sugar cookies, as though he made this sort of deal every day of his life. She had a fierce impulse to snatch the refreshments away from him.

She scrutinized his handsome face, looking for any sign of gloating. That she found none did not mollify her, and unpleasant emotions swirled inside her like a maelstrom. She focused all of her attention on making out a receipt, determined not to reveal her distress. It would be the utmost humiliation. Drawing in one shaky breath and then another, she struggled to get a grip on herself as she debated how to handle this situation.

Like the professional businesswoman she was, she scolded herself. What else could she do but act polite? Why give him the additional satisfaction of seeing her behave in any other manner? She had more pride than that!

"Here you are," she said, crisply handing him the slip of paper where she had meticulously recorded all of his purchases.

Taking a firm grip on herself, she moved her lips into a friendly, if perhaps stiff, smile. She looked up and met his gaze directly. His amber eyes were suddenly full of good humor. He didn't even have the manners to look uncomfortable about what he had just pulled off.

"By the way," she said, "welcome to the neighborhood."

"Thank you." His mouth quirked upward at one corner as an expression of admiration came over his face. "You're a good sport, Roseanna MacAuly. I think I'm going to like you as much as I liked your aunt."

Roseanna flushed. Then, as his smile warmed her,

she found her raging emotions calming down and her normal common sense returning. She knew it was unreasonable to be angry with Simon, for he had done nothing more than be a great customer. She had no one to blame but herself for not being more careful about her pricing.

She cleared her throat. "Yes, well, you've certainly made my day most interesting."

He finished his second cookie and brushed off his hands. "I'd like the furniture brought over as soon as possible. I'll be having my own grand-opening sale at the end of the month."

"So soon?" Roseanna was surprised. "Didn't you say you just bought the business?"

"Three weeks ago."

Come to think of it, she had noticed a lot of activity across the street. There had been a painter's truck and another for a sign maker. An oval board with *Oakes Antiques* painted in gold and flanked by silhouettes of oak trees, identical to his business card, had been placed above a new forest-green canvas awning. A third truck had come loaded with lawn maintenance equipment and plants. By the end of that day the strip of yard in front of the store had been transformed from a nondescript patch of sorrowful turf to a well-tended garden, complete with three flowering cherry saplings and lush groupings of yellow daffodils.

No wonder Simon would get his store going so quickly. It appeared as though he could afford to hire all the help he needed, while Roseanna struggled by on her own, or with the occasional help of Tim and Karyn.

"I have a man who delivers for me. Is tomorrow night soon enough?" she asked, proud of herself for keeping her tone so professional when she still felt shaky.

"That would be fine." He wished her luck on her sale, and on his way out the door lifted the oak watchmaker's cabinet into his arms as though the sturdy piece weighed nothing, and was gone.

Roseanna leaned against the back wall of her store and suppressed a yawn. It was late Sunday afternoon and with the excitement of the sale nearly over her energy level had plummeted. What an exhausting but exhilarating time it had been!

Though the weather had held, she had not had as many shoppers as yesterday, but enough to feel satisfied. Now the courtyard was deserted, and in the store only one customer remained. Missy Calhoun, an old classmate of Roseanna's, had arrived just before closing time and was now scrutinizing a wicker baby carriage with a missing wheel.

"Do you have the wheel for this thing?" Missy asked with a frown, taking her time examining the item. She was as skinny as ever, and as well dressed, today in a sleek pink suit.

"I'm sorry. I don't."

"Too bad." Missy abandoned the carriage and began picking through a display of aging kitchen appliances. She held up an avocado-colored electric can opener and released the same screechy giggle that had made Roseanna's skin crawl ever since kindergarten. "I've got to get this thing as a gag gift. It's just awful! Does it work?"

"I'll plug it in for you." When it just sat there, a dead lump of metal, Roseanna shrugged to hide her embarrassment. She thought she had tested everything to make sure there were no problems. "I guess not."

"Junk for the junk store." Missy giggled.

Roseanna clenched her teeth, determined to remain pleasant and unruffled. Surely Missy would leave soon.

Missy dusted her manicured fingers, causing her large diamond rings to sparkle in the harsh store lights. Her cupid's-bow mouth puckered into an expression of distaste. "This is quite a place you've got here, Roseanna," she said, her sarcasm thinly veiled.

"Do you have a career?" Roseanna inquired, hoping against hope Missy was working at some lowly position.

"Oh, no. I married a doctor," she chirped. "I suppose I don't need the money like you do."

"I enjoy the challenge of being a business owner," Roseanna shot back.

Missy arched one sharply penciled brow. "I just remembered! Weren't you always talking about someday having a clothing boutique?" Before Roseanna had time to respond, she giggled again and continued, "Oh well, a secondhand shop suits you better. You've certainly got the right name for it, Secondhand Rose."

Fiery heat erupted in her cheeks. "I *will* have the clothing store one day," Roseanna countered with angry conviction.

At the maddening smirk of disbelief on Missy's

face, it was all Roseanna could do to keep from escorting her bodily out the front door. She had disliked Missy Marie Calhoun as a child, and as a grown woman she still found her as irritating as a mosquito.

In school Roseanna had been smarter than Missy. In retaliation, Missy—the spoiled only child of the town's most well-heeled citizen—and her select clique had tormented Roseanna. She was Secondhand Rose to them, and they had taken great sport in pointing out every flaw they claimed they saw in her outfits. Often their cruel teasing had driven her to hide in the school bathroom where she would try desperately to stifle her tears.

"Roseanna?" She heard Tim's familiar masculine voice call out from the front of the store.

"Back here," she replied over her shoulder, grateful for the interruption.

When she saw Tim she gasped. The stocky young man who was her part-time helper limped toward her supported by a crutch, and had a bandage wrapped around his ankle.

"Tim! What happened?"

"I'll tell you later. Say, aren't you supposed to close at five?" he asked in a loud voice. "It's a quarter past now."

Blinking in surprise, Missy checked her gold watch. "Oh, you want to go home for the night. I'm so sorry, Roseanna. I was having so much fun I didn't realize the time. Call me if you ever really get that clothing store. I think that's more my style," she offered a parting shot as the three of them made their way to the front.

Blood pounding in her temples, Roseanna debated sending her old enemy off with a scathing comment of her own. But a glance at Tim's bemused expression calmed her down. If she could handle someone like Simon Oakes in a professional manner, it should be simple to deal with Missy Calhoun. Running a secondhand store, with all the difficulties that entailed, was good practice for whatever business endeavors would be in her future, she reminded herself.

"Good-bye," Roseanna said crisply, rising to her self-imposed challenge. "It's been very interesting seeing you again." *There, that was quite satisfactory,* Roseanna complimented herself.

After Missy had at last departed, Roseanna gratefully turned the OPEN sign to its CLOSED side. The courtyard was still full of merchandise that had to be brought in.

"Thanks for giving her the big hint. I didn't know how to get rid of her," Roseanna said to Tim, who had joined her at the door. She puffed out a long sigh of relief and ran her hands through her hair.

"Who was that?"

She shuddered. "A nightmare from my childhood."

Tim leaned against the doorframe, his tie-dyed T-shirt creating a wild splash of color. He was actually two years younger than Roseanna, but his bulky physique and wire-rimmed glasses made him appear older than he was.

He ran a hand through his unruly cap of blond hair and sighed. "You need to be more assertive."

"I know," she replied, thinking again of Simon. "I'm practicing."

She pointed at where his grubby jeans were rolled up to expose the freshly wrapped ankle. "Tim, are you going to tell me what you did to yourself?"

"After we finished setting up the sale this morning I went hiking. I wanted to do some landscape painting. Like the clumsy oaf I am, I slipped and gave my ankle a real good twisting. Ruined the canvas I'd just spent the entire afternoon working on, too." His expression clouded over. "I'm afraid I'm not going to be much help bringing in the stuff tonight. I've left you in a bind, I know. And me, too. I need some rent money real bad."

"Don't worry, I'll lend you some."

"Thanks. You know I'm good for it."

She was glad Tim felt better, but her own mood had sunk down to the floor. She gazed dispiritedly at the sale merchandise outside. It would take her hours to get everything inside by herself. And how would she manage the heavy pieces of furniture? What a mess!

"I'll try calling Karyn."

She went inside to phone and was on her way back out again when she heard Tim speaking to someone, another man it sounded like.

"The store is closed," Tim's voice boomed out. "You'll have to come back on Tuesday."

"Where's Roseanna?" came a firm response.

Tim straightened to block the entrance. He seemed to have the ability to expand his chest like a cock preparing to fight, and she was forced to peer around his shoulder to see Simon Oakes.

Standing on the porch with his arms folded casually across his chest, Simon exuded an aura of quiet authority that Tim, with all his youthful blustering, failed to match. Dressed today in khaki trousers and an ivory sweater under his dark jacket, he looked more handsome than ever.

"Excuse me, Tim," she murmured, squeezing past his bulk.

"Roseanna, hello again." Simon's soft deep voice wrapped around her, affecting her in a way Tim's gruff tone never had. His gaze held hers for a lingering moment.

"Simon, this is Tim Anderson. He worked for my aunt and now assists me off and on," she said, and followed up by introducing Simon.

"I'll bet he was supposed to help you move your merchandise inside," Simon quickly assessed the situation.

"Yep," she said with a disheartened sigh.

Tim gave her back a comforting pat, his hand remaining there. "Did you get hold of your friend?"

She frowned. "No."

Simon observed them closely, as though he were drawing conclusions about their relationship. "I'll help you out tonight, Roseanna."

She felt suddenly, inexplicably prickly. "There's no need. I'll manage." His amber eyes, as dark now as the evening sky, bore into hers. "I'd be happy to do it," he insisted. "What are neighbors for?"

"Seems to me you two will soon be in competition with each other," Tim noted, his jaw jutting outward ever so slightly.

Roseanna heard the warning in Tim's voice for her

to suspect Simon's motives and not let down her guard.

"I don't think that will be a problem," Simon answered coolly. He seemed unflappable. "The two stores are very different."

"That's for sure," Roseanna agreed. Last night after her own shop was closed she had crossed the street to peer into Simon's windows. From what she could see, he would be selling expensive, genuine antiques while she dealt in yesterday's castoffs.

"I believe we'll complement each other." Simon removed his jacket and laid it on the porch, bringing an end to the discussion. "Shall we get started?"

"Oh, all right. I'd be grateful," she acquiesced. "Thanks for coming by, Tim. You had better go home and rest that leg." She watched him ease himself off the doorframe, obviously reluctant to leave. "Really, go on," she dismissed him. "I'm okay now."

Before Tim even made it out of the courtyard, Simon had rolled up his sleeves and gotten down to business. "Do you need to change?" His gaze swept admiringly over her slacks and blouse outfit.

"I'm fine."

"It's cool out here. You'd better grab a jacket."

"Okay."

"And bring your hand truck," he said, his tone brisk. "We'll start with the heavier pieces."

"Aye, aye, Captain," Roseanna quipped tartly under her breath as she turned to head inside.

"I heard that."

She spun around, starting to turn pink. "Don't think me ungrateful—"

"But you're captain of the ship here?" He nodded toward her sign. "And if I don't watch my step I might feel the sharp edge of a cutlass?" A brow arched, and his voice took on a teasing quality as he added, "Or do you find other ways to torture men who don't please you?"

Roseanna did not think it was possible for her face to get any hotter, but by the feel of the fire in her cheeks she knew she must be glowing like embers. Why did this man affect her like no other?

She hurried inside. Simon was right; the air had become crisply cool with the coming night. After slipping on a warm coat, she retrieved the hand truck and pushed it over to a chest of drawers with a worn coat of orange paint.

"Now that we have our rank sorted out," she quipped, "would you care to assist me with this lovely item?"

Working together in a companionable and efficient way, they finished the job in little more than half an hour. Simon had considered taking the merchandise he had purchased that morning over to his own store, but decided against it when he saw Roseanna slump down onto the steps. She looked beat. Letting her rest, he removed the ramp they had used to roll the furniture onto the porch and stored it next to the building.

"Are you ready to close up?" he asked, wheeling the hand truck inside.

She stretched and yawned. "All that's left is to take your things over."

"Have you eaten?"

"I had a sandwich."

"For lunch, I'll bet." He checked his watch. "Probably about five or six hours ago."

She shrugged, realizing what he was getting at and not sure how she felt about it.

"Forget about my purchases for tonight. I'm going to take you out and feed you." He held out his hands to her and when she grasped them began gently helping her to her feet.

"Ouch!" she yelped.

He released her at once, concern written all over his face. "What is it? What's wrong?"

Frowning, she examined her palm. "I think I got a splinter from that last cabinet we moved."

"Let me see." He reached for her hand, this time being careful where he touched, and tried to find the hurt spot. "It's too dark out here, even under the porch light," he said, scowling. "We'll have to go in and take care of this."

Roseanna shuddered, glaring at the offending hand. "I hate splinters. I used to let my mom pull them out while I squeezed my eyes shut and pretended not to know what was going on."

"Do you have tweezers and antiseptic here?"

"I keep a first-aid kit in the bathroom at the back of the store." She grimaced in resignation. "I suppose I'd better go get it over with."

"I'll come with you."

"I'm a big girl now. I think I can manage."

"Humor me," he insisted with a stubborn set to his mouth. "I want to make sure you're all right."

"Suit yourself. But I'm warning you, I may

scream," she threatened, half-smiling. She slipped her hand out of his and headed inside.

Aware of the man trailing behind her through the cramped aisles, she wished the store looked better. Even with all her efforts to clean and organize, the space looked shabby and crowded to her.

Recalling her conversation with Missy, Roseanna felt an even sharper distaste for her surroundings. A secondhand store was the last business she would have wanted for herself. She hated used things! Yet even though she did not want her great-aunt's shop and planned to sell it, she had decided it was smart to first get the place fixed up and running smoothly.

The bathroom, at least, pleased her. It gleamed from a new coat of paint—bright yellow—and had been scrubbed spotless. She had decorated it with fun things she'd found in the store. A Japanese paper lantern hung from the ceiling, a ceramic shell held a bar of soap, and a bright print of a tropical island framed in bamboo graced one wall.

Roseanna took the items she needed from the medicine cabinet and settled down on a stool to work. The splinter had gone in deep and it throbbed painfully. She was gritting her teeth, preparing herself mentally, when Simon relieved her of the tweezers.

"I'll do it. I had three little sisters to take care of."

He crouched next to her, brushing against her leg in the cramped space. The small bathroom was not designed for two—especially if one was over six feet tall. The intimate atmosphere made her uncomfortable and fidgety.

Simon glowered at her. "I can't do this if you're squirming around. You're worse than Madeline."

Roseanna perked up. "Who's that?"

"Youngest sister. A real hellion." He concentrated on positioning the tweezers. "Now, be still."

"I'm trying. This makes me nervous."

"In that case, close your eyes," he ordered.

Losing her nerve, she snatched her hand away. "Oh, Simon, I don't think—"

He caught it and opened her clenched fingers with admirable patience. His firm grip made it clear he intended to have his way. "Do as I say, and I'll have this out before you can count to three."

"One," she snapped, lowering her eyelids. He leaned heavily against her, causing a reaction that completely diverted her attention. Before she had managed to get herself together enough to say "two" she felt a tug, and heard him announce, "It's done."

"Thank you," she said simply as he rose to his feet. He stepped back into the doorway, where he paid careful attention while she applied the antiseptic ointment and a bandage to the small wound. "It feels better already."

"Now let's go eat," he said.

This time she didn't even attempt to argue with him. She was too tired and too hungry and too curious about her handsome neighbor. "Good, I'm starved. But I'm paying."

After waiting for her to shut off the lights and secure the building, he led her across the street to where his dark-green van was parked in front of his store.

The van's side had been painted with a sign that matched the one on the storefront.

"You've been very kind," she said.

He retrieved his keys from his jacket pocket. "Is that what you call it when you've been taken advantage of?"

"What are you talking about?"

"Yesterday morning." He unlocked the passenger door and helped her in. "You undersold your antiques. If I'd had more decency I would have told you so instead of taking advantage of the situation."

"That's true!" She narrowed her eyes at him. "Are you a rogue by nature?"

"I might be a rogue, but I did you a favor."

"Ha! I suppose you're going to tell me you taught me a lesson."

"Roseanna." Her name rolled out like a gentle caress. "You're in business. If you don't know what you're doing, then shame on you. I suspect you'll be more careful from now on."

"Darn right I will," she shot back.

Simon joined her in the truck and turned on the ignition, then paused as though something were troubling him. "By the way, I caught the whopper you told about the table. The way you and your girlfriend worked together was a professional job. I hope you don't intend to continue to conduct yourself that way."

"Now wait just one darned second!" she sputtered in outrage. "That story about the table was absolutely true."

He quirked a brow. "And your girlfriend?"

"I had hoped you hadn't witnessed that little epi-

sode. I know it looked bad." She drew in long breath
as she tried to think how to explain. For some reason,
it was very important that Simon understand. "I don't
suppose you have any reason to believe me, since we
hardly know each other, but I don't tell lies to sell
things, and I don't manipulate my customers. I just
don't do business that way. I guess my only excuse is
that Karyn caught me off guard with her game, and I
didn't know how stop her. I did have a talk with her
about it. I made it clear she was never to 'help' me
that way again."

"I'm glad to hear that," he said, nodding in approval. "No harm was done, anyway," he added in her
defense. "The woman wanted the table. She would
have bought it no matter what."

"You believe me?"

"Of course."

She frowned at him suspiciously. "Still, that was a
very mean accusation."

He leveled his gaze on hers. "I needed to clear the
air. It was on my mind."

She eyed him curiously. "Why would you care?"

His expression became veiled. "I wanted to know if
the competition was dishonest."

"I'm probably more honest than your grandmother,"
she retorted tartly, still smarting from his comments.

He grinned, and wisecracked, "Ah, but you don't
know my grandmother."

A smile came to her lips, unbidden. How was it that
this man could rile her one moment, then charm her
the next? "Lucky for you, I don't hold grudges."

"Indeed." Devilment returned to his eyes. "I'd hate

to have a lady pirate across the street entertaining visions of revenge."

As he drove them out of town he tried to peer at his attractive red-haired companion out of the corner of his eye. Although she rested against the back of the seat in a relaxed pose, he had the distinct impression all of her senses were on alert. She was wary of him, and had a right to be so. Roseanna reminded him of a sassy little cat.

And a smart one. Despite her mistake in pricing, she was obviously as bright as she was pretty. She wouldn't allow him to get the best of her a second time.

Not that he would want to.

She straightened and looked around. "Where are we going?"

"The Water's Edge."

"Oh, I love it there," she enthused, her simple expression of delight making him feel wonderful. "It's so fun and lively. I'm so tired that at a quiet place I would probably be snoring in about ten minutes."

They reached the rustic waterfront restaurant in a few more minutes and found a seat—a bench, actually. The entire place consisted of a bar and picnic tables lined up in rows, end to end. There was also a covered porch overlooking the water for when the weather was warm enough to dine outside. Simon settled Roseanna first, then slid in alongside her, resting his arms on the brown butcher paper that covered the table. She immediately began studying the blackboard for the evening's specials.

Once they had ordered, there was a comfortable lull

in their conversation. The pleasant sound of talking and laughter swirled around them. For a Sunday night the place was busy, filled with families and tourists. At the table beside them a small boy stuffed himself with crab, smearing his face in the process. Simon caught Roseanna's eye and they both chuckled at the sight.

"Do you have siblings, too?" Simon asked.

"Three, like you. A brother and two sisters. They're all older than me."

"I'd like to have a large family one day."

Appearing almost wistful, Roseanna's gaze remained on the child. "Me too." Her expression became serious. "That is, if I can afford them. My kids aren't going to grow up like I did."

Their conversation was interrupted by a chatty middle-aged waitress who brought them each a glass of white wine. After taking a sip, Roseanna looked over at him and smiled. The color of her eyes was a sparkling blue that reminded him of sailing in the Caribbean. They were the kind of eyes that could lead a man into paradise.

Or into dangerous waters.

Simon maneuvered his gaze away. "How did your opening-day sale go?"

"Great, except for being worried the whole time that I had underpriced everything."

The idea that he had caused her to suffer bothered him. Yesterday morning she had been simply another shopkeeper, a stranger. Now she had become . . . more. He clamped down on his wandering thoughts, unwilling to explore further in that direction.

"I grabbed most of the real bargains," he informed her. "At least among your antiques. I don't know much about secondhand merchandise."

Her expression softened. "Apparently a lot of other people thought I had good deals, because I did better than I had expected. I'm really quite pleased."

"I'm glad for you." He reached over to take her hand in his, squeezing it gently. "I have the distinct feeling that with you at the helm, Treasures will be a big success."

"It's certainly not my dream store. But since it is what I have, the least I can do is spruce it up a bit. I really don't know what else to do with it. It's just an old junk shop."

"I think there are a lot of possibilities," Simon responded, his interest piqued. Roseanna might be inexperienced in business but she had a good head on her shoulders, and with her plucky spirit he had no doubt she could achieve anything she wished—if only her heart were in it. Having a competitor snatch up all her bargains must have left a sour taste in her mouth for the secondhand business and undermined her confidence in herself, even if she did pretend otherwise.

He toyed with his fork, thinking things over. He had nothing to be ashamed of in his dealings with her and yet, here he was, being steadily pricked by guilt. And he knew the reason why. It was because over the course of the last few hours his relationship with Roseanna had changed, and he didn't make it a habit of getting the better of his friends.

"Roseanna, look," he blurted out, startling himself as much as her. "I want cancel our deal. You can return my money and keep your merchandise. You can easily resell everything at a much higher price."

"What?" She scowled at him.

"Yeah, let's just call off the whole thing off." He was surprised at the sweet feeling of relief that swept through him. "Just forget it."

She was shaking her head. "Your purchase was completely aboveboard. I don't hold it against you."

"Sure, but . . ." The look of fierce pride flashing in her eyes warned him not to continue. He shrugged, seeing from the expression on her face there was no way he was going to convince her to take her merchandise back, and liking her all the more for it. "Suit yourself."

"I will. Thanks for the offer, though. That was very gentlemanly of you." After a moment her face softened, and she added, "You know, Simon, if someone had to teach me a lesson, I'm kind of glad it was you."

He laughed. "That's finished, then."

"Yes."

"No. Not quite. Be forewarned. I intend to make it up to you."

Curiosity lit her eyes. "Oh? Just what did you have in mind?"

"I don't know yet," he replied with a wink.

Their meal arrived, and Roseanna let Simon order a second glass of wine for her. For a while they were both busy dismantling the steaming crabs that had been brought to them in cardboard trays. She turned the conversation to impersonal topics and found she enjoyed hearing Simon's thoughts and opinions, even though she didn't agree with all of them. He was well informed and made a fascinating dinner companion.

When they finished and the table was cleared, they lingered over a cup of strong, aromatic coffee. It was near closing time when he finally escorted her out into the quiet night. Before opening the door of his van for her he reached into his pants pocket.

"I nearly forgot—the reason I came over this evening."

She grinned. "I thought it was to rescue a damsel in distress."

"No, you just got lucky on that score." He dangled a diamond-and-emerald heart-shaped necklace that sparkled in the parking area lights. "I found this in one of the drawers of the watchmaker's cabinet. I thought it must have been left there accidentally."

"Oh, Simon." She gasped, her hand flying to her lips. "That was Aunt Tildy's favorite necklace. She must have hidden it in the cabinet. She was eccentric like that, squirreling her treasures away in odd places."

"In the store?"

"I haven't discovered anything there yet. I did find things in her apartment above the shop, where I'm staying now. There was money and jewelry in dresser drawers, under the bed, and even in her sugar bowl. Nothing very significant . . . but I always wondered if there might be more somewhere." She fingered the necklace, feeling its sharp edges in her palm. "I cleared all of her old things out of the apartment, including the watchmaker's cabinet. I tried checking all fifty drawers, but a few were stuck. I didn't hear any rattling noises, so I assumed it was empty."

"It had been wrapped in a handkerchief," he explained, stepping closer. "I guess this belongs to you now." He lifted the jewelry to her neck, tunneling beneath her hair to fasten the clasp. Then he leaned back and gazed at her, nodding his approval. "It suits you. It's perfect with your red hair."

Warming under his attentions, she looked up into his face, unreadable and mysterious now. "You purchased the cabinet, so rightfully the necklace is yours."

"So it is," he agreed solemnly. "Now I'm giving it to you." At her expression of protest he added, "This isn't business. Please accept it."

"Oh, Simon. How can I ever thank you?"

"I can only think of one way." His deep voice captured her in a web of sensuality. She stood, helpless to resist, as his hands cradled her face and his mouth covered hers.

Chapter Three

"Roseanna, wake up."

Roseanna opened her eyes with a start and sat up straight, looking around in an attempt to get her bearings. She was still in Simon's van, and they were parked in front of her store. Light from the corner street lamp softly illuminated the planes of his handsome face.

"I can't believe I dozed off," she murmured, feeling embarrassed.

He reached over and smoothed a wisp of hair off her cheek. "I'm not surprised. I'll bet you've been up since before dawn getting the sale merchandise outside. You were already exhausted before I let you have all that wine."

She raised her brows at him. "You let me? What kind of statement is that? You let me." She shook her

37

head in mock disgust. "I don't believe I'm hearing talk like that from a modern man." Despite herself, she yawned broadly.

"Who says I'm a modern man?" he retorted, the husky challenge in his voice capturing her attention.

His hooded eyes, the intimate enclosure of the van, her sleepiness . . . it was all working on her senses, making her feel caught and helpless in a delicious blanket of sensuality. Her heart thumped away as she waited in suspended time for whatever he might do next. When he leaned in her direction she swayed to meet him, her lips parting and her eyes drifting closed.

She heard him clear his throat. Before her eyelids had even snapped open again she could feel him moving away, the space between them growing larger and cooler.

By the time she was able to focus, he was jerking the keys from the ignition. "I'll walk you to your door," he offered.

Roseanna grabbed her purse and fumbled with the door latch. Simon escorted her beneath the dogwoods and through the well-lit courtyard to a door at the corner of the building, which she unlocked to reveal a flight of stairs up to her apartment

"Good night," she said, feeling unsure of what to do next.

Simon seemed to have no such problem. He immediately bent to brush her lips with a kiss.

A gust of wind rattled the old windows of her store, startling Roseanna as she searched under the worn cushions of her aunt's gold-and-green floral sofa. All day Monday a storm had been brewing, the unsettled weather reflecting her inward restlessness. Finding nothing on top of the sofa, she got down on her knees and tapped the springs underneath with a broom handle, all the while trying to keep her mind on her task instead of on the feelings Simon had aroused in her.

The kisses the evening before had been brief, almost inconsequential. Yet, as casual as they had been, they affected her on some deep, mysterious level. She had to admit that she liked Simon Oakes and found him extremely attractive. Part of her yearned to throw caution to the wind, and yet, he was a neighbor, and a competitor, as Tim had pointed out. Things could become very uncomfortable. Perhaps it would be unwise to go beyond a simple friendship. Next time she saw him, she decided, she would exhibit more control over herself.

Giving herself a mental pat on the back for being so sensible, she turned her attention back to her task. She clicked off her light, rose to her feet, and brushed off the knees of her jeans. The last of her great-aunt's furnishings to be searched was an overstuffed plaid chair with doilies covering the holes in the arms. So far she had not come up with anything but a few coins, hairpins, and dust balls.

The three grandfather clocks lined up behind the great, hulking desk that housed her cash register ticked away the minutes. It was nearly four in the afternoon. Karyn had promised to come by after work and help take Simon's purchases over to him, since an earlier call to Tim confirmed he was still out of commission.

She knew Simon was at his store because she had

seen lights on and activity inside. Often throughout the long afternoon she found herself staring across the street and wondering if he might come over or call. But he had not.

Thunder rumbled, vibrating through her bones, and the clouds finally burst, sending down waves of rain. The cold wind seemed able to find every crack in the bricks and boards of the old building. She finished with the chair and left empty-handed to pour herself a cup of coffee from the automatic pot she kept on a table nearby. She was thus occupied when she heard something strange. She cocked her head, listening.

Plink, plunk, plink, plunk.

"Oh, darn it all!" she complained out loud, setting her cup down hard enough to slosh the contents over the rim. She knew that sound. The roof on the small side room was leaking.

Old Mr. Peterson, her endearing but unreliable land-lord, had promised to patch the bad spots. He had as-sured her with all his octogenarian charm that he would accomplish this feat himself, no less. She had wondered at the time how he was going to manage, since he needed a cane to get around. Had she really believed he could climb a ladder and crawl about on a sloped roof? She hurried to confirm her suspicions.

Peering into the room, she saw drops accumulating on the water-stained ceiling. They grew fatter and fat-ter until they could hold their weight no longer, then plopped to the floor. The 1950s-style black-and-white linoleum gleamed from their efforts. *Don't worry about it,* she told herself firmly, not about to let this latest frustration get her down. The day was coming when things would change. She would have a store that only sold brand-spanking-new merchandise, and it would be housed in a building that certainly would not leak. Someday, she reminded herself, she would have no more worries in her life.

Kicking off her moccasins to keep them from getting soiled, Roseanna tiptoed inside and gasped at the cold, wet sensation. Quickly she pushed the mismatched assortment of chairs and tables out of the way. Then she raced back through the store, grabbing anything that would hold water. Returning to the room with her load, she sank into a crouch and duck-walked across the floor, arranging pots as she went. A chilly drop landed between her eyes and snaked its way down her nose. As she leaned forward to position a pan, tendrils of hair stuck to the wet spot. Another drip fell on her neck, slid beneath her sweater, and ran down her neck. She shoved a crockpot against a roaster and they collided like bumper cars, the clang ringing in her ears.

Banging noises greeted Simon as he came in out of the storm, closing the door firmly behind him. He shook cold rainwater from the collar of his jacket and surveyed the store. The racket ceased and, except for the melodious ticking of the grandfather clocks, there was silence. The air contained the pleasant smell of coffee and something lemony, like furniture polish. There was no sign of the cute shopkeeper.

A clattering sound broke the quiet. Following the direction of the noise, he came to a side room. As he approached, a flash of Roseanna's distinctive hair caught his eye, and he halted in the doorway. The slender woman knelt on the floor, her back to him. She balanced a saucepan in one hand and a dog bowl in the other. Her gaze was trained on the ceiling. He could hear her muttering to herself—something about decrepit buildings and unreliable landlords.

She obviously had not heard him arrive. It did not take long before the fat bead of moisture she had been eyeing fell, and she shoved the dog bowl beneath it.

"Got you!" she exclaimed in triumph.

Simon leaned against the doorjamb, the heavy book he was carrying tucked under his arm, and clapped. "Good catch."

She whirled to face him, lost her balance, and sat down hard on the wet floor. The metal pan she had been holding skidded noisily across the linoleum.

"I really hate it when people sneak up on me," she snapped, lifting a hand from the floor and shaking water from it. Despite her scolding, the happy sparkle in her eyes assured him of his welcome.

Her thick mane of hair cascaded over her shoulders to frame her cheeks with rich russet color. She had the face of an angel, he mused, with a fanciful turn of thought. Her wide-eyed schoolgirl appearance would help her in her work. He had bargained with vendors from Mexico City to Rome, and if they had one thing in common, it was their deceptively innocent appearance. A shopkeeper could look as saintly as Mother Teresa, yet try to sell "genuine antiquities" that had been made the day before—and at sky-high prices. Saturday morning, he had been ready to include Rose-

anna in that category, but now his heart assured him
she was as sincere as she appeared.

His heart? He balked at the thought, but it was true.
Already this fiery-haired female had him entranced.
And he didn't like it. Not one bit.

When she started to rise, he automatically stepped
into the room and reached out to assist her. Her grip
felt cold and damp, yet soft and strong, pulsing with
vitality.

Moving awkwardly in an effort to avoid brushing
against him, she slipped through the doorway and
gathered up a pair of moccasins.

"How was business today?" he asked casually as he
followed her to the massive oak front desk.

"I'm closed on Monday," she answered politely.
"I'm just here doing a little cleaning and straightening."

In a stiff, nervous motion, she sat in the desk chair
and swung one leg over the other. His gaze roved upward from her form-fitting jeans to the fuzzy turquoise
sweater that clung to her body. She wasn't wearing
the heart necklace. Instead, a Jolly Roger pendant dangled from a chain.

As Roseanna slipped on her shoes, she covertly observed Simon, in his navy blue jacket and his dark
hair wet with rain. A drop fell from a brown curl and
made a crooked trail down his forehead. She followed
its progress until she could stand it no longer.

"I'll be right back," she told him, pushing herself
up. She hurried to the restroom and returned with a
towel.

Simon accepted the offering, wiped his face and

neck, and then vigorously rubbed his head. Seized by the intimacy of the moment, she felt an unfathomable closeness to this man she barely knew.

As though he intended to stay a while, Simon removed his jacket and hung it on the back of a wobbly Mission chair. She could not help but notice how his blue denim shirt brought out the golden highlights in his hazel eyes.

"I suppose you're wondering when I intended to bring over your purchases," she said, trying to bring her wayward thoughts back to safe territory. "I have a friend who is coming to help me after she gets off work in an hour. I hope that fits your schedule."

He shrugged as if it were of little concern. "That's fine. I'll help, too. If it's still pouring we'll postpone until tomorrow."

"You're a man of great pity," she said, smiling at him in relief.

He grinned back. "Very true. That's why I came over. I wanted to show you something." He handed her a thick softcover book.

"Bailey's Antique Prices," she read the title, then glanced up at him questioningly. "What's this for?"

"It's for you. I have another, so I don't need it."

She thumbed through it. "I guess you're saying I do?" Their gazes met.

"If you want to make any money in this game, you do," he said with conviction.

She closed the book with a decisive thump. "It's very thoughtful of you, but I don't have any more real antiques. All of this stuff is just"—she wrinkled her nose—"used."

"Are you certain of that?"

She hesitated. "Yes. I think so."

"You don't sound so sure."

"I haven't seen anything that seemed old enough to be worth much," she said, this time with more conviction.

"That's because you don't know what to look for. I bet I can find some treasures here you didn't even know you had," he challenged.

"Is that right?" she tossed back, intrigued but dubious.

"I'll bet you a cup of coffee I do."

"You're on." She waved a hand around the room. "The place is yours, sir."

For a long moment Simon stood unmoving, his gaze roaming the territory. Then, like a hound on a scent, she saw his attention hone in on a shelf holding several oil lamps and electric table lamps.

"Right there," he said with triumphant excitement in his voice. He walked over and pulled out a small metal lantern that had been almost lost among the other items.

"Do you know what this is?" he asked, checking her price.

"Not more than the obvious."

"I thought so."

She sighed. "All right, go on, tell me."

"This is a miner's lantern," he informed her. "It would be hooked to the front of the miner's helmet. Inside the lantern water drips onto carbide to create a gas that burns, which makes light."

"Really? That's interesting."

"And you're practically giving it away. Try looking it up in the book."

She did so and squirmed. "Okay. That's one item."

He walked around, looking at things. "You have a lot of great stuff here."

"Really? It doesn't look like much to me. You should have seen the store before Aunt Tildy died. It was really packed. She must have sold off a lot toward the end."

He didn't have to go far to discover another antique. From behind a large group of glassware of various sorts where it was effectively hidden, he lifted a delicate china vase covered with tiny shamrocks. He raised his brows at her.

"No, I don't know anything about it," she admitted before he inquired. "It is pretty, though."

His brow arched. "It's Belleek." He turned it over to show her the bottom. "See that mark? That will tell you how old it is and thus how much it is worth."

She hated to ask. "Is that one old?"

He placed it gently into her hands. "Yes. Without having a pricing guide for this type of china, I would guess it's worth between one hundred and two hundred dollars."

It was a good thing Roseanna had a fair grip on the fragile piece, or else she might have dropped it in shock. She hastily removed her price sticker.

"Why didn't you grab these things on Saturday if they're such great deals?" she wanted to know.

He grinned. "I had a guilty conscience?"

"I doubt it," she responded with a snort.

He puffed out a sigh, admitting, "You're right. The

truth is, I was in a hurry. At the time I suspected I could find more here but I had an appointment, and I was already late. And I had made plans to be out of town most of Sunday. When I came by last night, I had only just returned." His expression became concerned. "I'm sorry to tell you this, but I imagine the antique hunters have probably already scoured your place. I'm surprised they missed these things."

Jabs of hot anger stabbed her, followed by a flush of embarrassment. In pretense of studying the vase, she lowered her gaze away from his discerning eyes. "I feel so foolish."

"Water under the bridge," he downplayed her mistakes in a matter-of-fact tone. "Now you know better."

"It doesn't matter anyway," Roseanna told him, trying to soothe her wounded pride. "I intend to sell this place soon."

"What? Why?"

Hearing the surprise in his voice, she shrugged and explained, "You see, I don't like old stuff. I never wanted a secondhand store."

"That's too bad. I can see it needs more work, but eventually this shop could be wonderful." He cast a glance around, as if sizing up the opportunity. "The building is spacious and picturesque. All it would take is someone with energy and imagination, both of which I suspect you possess in great quantity."

Mixed emotions swirled her thoughts into confusion, making Roseanna wish she hadn't brought up the topic. How could Simon ever understand her feelings? Just to make sure, she asked pointedly, "Did you grow up poor?"

"My family was well-off." He scrutinized her, as if trying to read her mind. She could almost see his keen intelligence gleaming from those intense golden eyes. "I get the picture; Miss Secondhand Rose."

"Don't call me that," she snapped, crossing her arms, and narrowed her eyes at him. "I loathe people calling me that."

"Ah, I get it," he said, winking at her frown. "You grew up with hand-me-downs, patches on your knees, and worn-out furniture." He waited until she gave him a curt nod before concluding, "And now you want better."

"And just what's wrong with that?" she tossed back.

"It wasn't a judgment." He opened his hands in an expression of innocence. "Simply an observation."

Roseanna immediately regretted letting her feelings out. All she had accomplished was to provide Simon an opportunity to poke fun at her. "Find one more genuine antique, and you'll get that cup of coffee," she challenged, returning to safer ground.

"I can taste it already." He smacked his lips playfully, then began to stroll around the store.

Roseanna remembered calling him a rogue. She had never met anyone so exactly fitting that description.

"Here's something," he said, picking up a bundle of old linens she had not paid much attention to. He handed them to her, the close proximity making her all too aware of his masculinity. He wore cologne. She could barely detect it, but it was there—a heady, manly scent that reminded her of the sea.

"Washed, ironed, and displayed nicely, these will

be a money-maker for you. Shall we continue?" he asked. "Or have I proved my point?"

"I concede."

He had given her another lesson that afternoon, and it had been a real eye-opener. Simon was a wealth of knowledge, and all she had to do was ask to have access to it.

"I would appreciate it if you'd search a little longer. I don't want to give anything else away—especially to an antiques dealer." She slapped her hand over her mouth, mortified. "Oh, how rude. I am sorry."

"No offense taken." He treated her to a wicked grin. "You do have to watch out for my type, you know. We take advantage of innocents like you."

Wondering just what he meant by that, she followed him as he made his way carefully through the store, pointing out a few more items. "I already have coffee on," she said when he finished. "You've earned it."

He eyed her consideringly. "I'm sure your brew is wonderful, but I know a great little coffeehouse I think you'll really enjoy."

She hesitated, recalling her decision to be cautious. "It's really pouring. Are you sure you want to go out in this?"

"You lost the bet," he reminded her. "Get your coat." He glanced toward the windows. It was dark and blowing hard. "And a very strong umbrella."

Roseanna chewed her lip. They were just friendly neighboring shopkeepers going out for a cup of coffee, she assured herself. It didn't mean anything more than that. "All right," she agreed. "I'll call Karyn and tell her not to come."

"Go ahead. I'm sure she'll appreciate it."

After she had locked the store, Simon grasped her hand in his firm grip and waited for a break in the rush-hour traffic before racing her across the street. They were both laughing and dripping by the time they made it into the dry safety of his van.

He was fun to be with, Roseanna mused, feeling more filled with life and joy than she could remember being for a long, long time. "Simon, I don't know if I could ever be as smart about antiques as you are," she said as she belted herself in. "I thought I had just inherited a neglected, boring secondhand store. Nothing to it."

He cocked his head as he thought that over. "It could be dull or it could be fantastic. It's all up to you, you know. That store can be whatever you make of it. You can create whatever you desire."

She knew exactly what he meant. Although she didn't want the shop, she couldn't help having intriguing, exciting ideas for it. She'd had to remind herself not to throw her heart into remodeling a store she did not intend to keep.

"How long have you been in the antiques business?" She studied his profile as they started down the road with the windshield wipers swishing back and forth on high speed. "You're so knowledgeable. It must be something you've done for years."

"Yes and no." He kept his eyes trained foreward, being careful on the slick rain-washed street.

"That clears it up," she quipped. She thought he would smile at that and was surprised when his mouth tightened instead.

"Yes, I know a lot about antiques and collectibles. I think I have always been fascinated with old things. And no, I haven't been in business long. In fact, this is my first store."

That surprised her. He seemed so utterly capable, while she sometimes felt just the opposite. Her attraction to this handsome, bedeviling man grew stronger by the moment. "What did you do before?" she asked, intrigued.

His frown deepened. "I owned an accounting firm with my wife."

"Wife?" Roseanna gaped at him.

"I'm sorry, ex-wife. We've been divorced almost a year now."

Chapter Four

Divorced. The word caused a sinking sensation in the pit of Roseanna's stomach. Like the used goods in her store, Simon was a secondhand man.

The stabbing ache of disappointment she felt surprised her. When had she become so interested in Simon? She cast a sideways glance at him, wondering about her unexpected feelings.

Divorced. She rolled the unsavory word around in her mind as she studied the stern line of his mouth. From his taut expression, she suspected he harbored bitter feelings over the end of his marriage. How long would it take him to heal? Would he ever? The answer was impossible to guess.

And it was not going to be her concern if she could help it. A shattered heart four years ago was lesson enough. Divorced men, *especially* newly divorced men, were now off-limits.

The coffeehouse was as charming as Simon had described it, a place she would normally have thoroughly enjoyed. But she consumed the full-bodied coffee without tasting a drop, and when Simon tried to entice her with one of the plump, glossy pastries in the deli case she shook her head, her stomach feeling like she had swallowed one of the old irons she sold in her shop. She managed to keep up her end of the conversation until a reasonable amount of time had passed, then politely insisted he take her home, inventing excuses for her eagerness to depart.

From his concerned, surreptitious glances she knew Simon suspected something was amiss, and was glad he didn't probe.

"Looks like we have a power outage," he broke into her gloomy mood as they drove down the unusually dark street toward their stores. The storm continued on unabated, as though it would last all night.

"I hope I have some candles." Roseanna stared out the side window, intent on keeping her gaze anywhere but on the man beside her. He pulled into the parking area of the unlit building, and before she could stop him he was out of the van and opening her door. They tried to share her red umbrella as they hurried to the door of her apartment, but with Simon stooping and her jumping puddles on tiptoe, it turned out be a ridiculous situation. Despite her unhappiness, Roseanna was smiling by the time they made it safely inside the entrance.

In the unbroken night all she could see of Simon was his shadowy form, but she felt his presence like a powerful masculine force crowding against her.

"Well, thanks for the coffee," she said awkwardly, as she folded the umbrella and set it in a corner. Looking upward at the eerie cavernous stairway, her pulse jumped and began to race.

"Will you be okay here?" Simon asked, the doubt in his voice making her even more nervous. "Are you afraid to go up in the dark?"

"I'm fine," she lied in a shaky, squeaky voice.

She sucked in a deep breath to calm herself. What a goose she was being. What was there to be scared of . . . besides the pitch-black rooms, the apartment she still did not feel quite at home in, the odd noises. She shuddered. She had always hated the dark.

Sometimes, late at night, she imagined she heard sounds downstairs. Bogeymen and ghosts. These were just silly, childish fears, she always assured herself. What she needed was less imagination and more mousetraps.

"There are bound to be some candles somewhere. . . ." Her hands felt icy, and she rubbed them together. Determinedly, she faced the stairs and reached for the railing. She tried to make her feet move onto the stair treads but they refused to cooperate. Her heart was banging so hard she thought for sure Simon must be able to hear it.

"Simon," she blurted out, unable to stop herself. "Would you mind going up with me?"

"I intended to anyway."

His calm, steady tone instantly bolstered her and a sweet relief flowed like honey through her veins.

He placed a hand on her waist as he stepped around her. "I'll head up first."

Immensely grateful, Roseanna followed his solid form up the stairway. At the top was another door that led into the apartment.

"It's not locked," she told him.

Reaching for her hand as casually as though he did it every day, Simon led her inside. With the blinds lowered, it was amazingly dark, and she gazed about, trying to get her bearings in the inky void. Just then she felt Simon's fingers squeeze hers in gentle reassurance, and she was glad for the comforting gesture, glad he was here with her.

"Where are your candles?" he asked.

"If I have any, they would be in the kitchen."

"Lead the way."

Thankful her place was rather sparse yet and they didn't have to worry about tripping over much furniture, Roseanna took Simon cautiously through the living room to the kitchen. Leaving him at the counter, she felt her way inside to search the drawers.

"Bingo! Got some." She found matches, too, and soon a cheerful pool of light spanned the distance between them. Simon was frowning.

"Roseanna, those are birthday candles."

"I know that," she returned in exasperation. "It's the best I could do." As she held one of the slim white candles she looked around for something to hold it. "Hand me that package of muffins."

Shaking his head at the ridiculous situation, Simon

pushed them over and watched as she implanted a candle in each of the four muffins.

"Shall we sing happy birthday now?" he quipped.

"You go ahead. I'll look for more candles."

Simon had to blow out and replace the precious candles twice while she ransacked all the drawers and cupboards. "Don't you have a flashlight?"

"I've been meaning to get one," she replied distractedly. "Look, I've found another box of birthday candles. Hey, these are the trick ones that won't blow out. They were for my sister, Evelyn's, birthday. You'd like her. She has a great sense of humor."

"Evelyn's going to get a good laugh when she hears about you sitting in the dark. Those candles are not going to last long."

Roseanna chewed on her lip. "I'll burn them one at a time. It will have to do. When they go out, I'll just head to bed."

Simon was shaking his head. "Come home with me. My place is across town. There might be power there."

Her heart began to pound again, this time from a very different kind of anxiety. She opened and closed her mouth, not knowing what to say. Considering her confused feelings about Simon, spending the night with him was much more frightening than her dark apartment.

Suddenly, an idea occurred to her. "I have lanterns downstairs," she said with a mixture of excitement and relief. "Do you remember? They are on the shelf with that miner's lamp. I know some of them have fuel." She snatched up a muffin, a handful of candles, and a box of matches. "I'm going down to get one. Are you coming?"

It took several of her candles to make it down and into the store. They found a large glass lantern filled with pink fuel and when Simon lit the wick, they grinned at each other as though they had achieved a great victory.

"You must think I'm a jerk, being afraid of the dark," she admitted, her good sense about remembering the lanterns having made her giddy with renewed self-confidence.

"I think you're quite brave."

"I'll just bet," she scoffed.

"No, honestly." The sincerity in his expression captivated her. "It's not easy running a business. Believe me, I know the headaches first-hand. You probably have friends and family who would help you out if you asked, but you're really on your own. I admire your independence and courage."

Roseanna reveled in the compliments. They infused her with a dizzy heat, as though she had imbibed a good long swallow of expensive brandy.

"Thank you," she murmured.

Simon's face, in the flickering light, had become a sculpture of angles that held her fascinated. Her gaze skimmed over his features and tousled damp hair. Although he exuded intelligence and worldly sophistication, there was nothing slick or snobbish about him. Along with nearly everything else about him, she found that very appealing.

They stood close. Way too close. She swallowed hard, her heart thumping away like a mad thing in her chest. When she met his eyes, dark with intensity, every sense she possessed heightened. The delicious memory of kisses they'd shared just the night before danced through her mind, and she licked her lips nervously. Gazing at him now, seeing in his eyes the same longing, she felt a powerful yearning to be swept into his strong embrace and just enjoy the bliss of the moment.

"Are you sure you'll be all right now?" he asked, his voice low and intimate.

Swallowing hard, she struggled to get a grip on herself. "Yes, yes of course." She stepped away from him, hoping his magnetic pull would lessen with distance. "I'll try my best to get your purchases over to you tomorrow," she said nervously. "What time would be good?"

"Seven-thirty. And forget about rounding up help. I'll come by, and we'll do it together."

In her current mood, Roseanna didn't think it safe to see him again so soon, but couldn't think of a way to refuse.

She locked the store behind them, and while Simon jogged through the rain to his van, she dashed to her apartment stairway door. From inside she watched him drive down the deserted street. Several minutes after his taillights disappeared from sight, she finally bolted the door and made her way up the stairs by lantern light.

Her heart still hammered and her thoughts spun. She had nearly kissed Simon again. Kissed him . . . She recalled with vivid clarity the moment of madness she had so narrowly escaped down in the store. Feeling flushed, she headed to a window and shoved it open. Several long minutes and deep breaths of cool, moist air later, she began to regain her equilibrium.

Simon Oakes. A powerful name for a powerful man. What was she going to do about him? He was divorced. She had promised herself never to become involved with a divorced man again.

Where had this need for the taste of his lips come from? And where had her sense of self-preservation gone? A powerful attraction had her in its grip. The trouble was, she felt it for the wrong man.

He had been married before and was, therefore, off limits. It was that simple.

She did not want a secondhand man. Somewhere out there was a man for her, a man who had not belonged to someone else. A man without scars on his heart she could never heal.

She thought of Gary and shivered, suddenly chilled. Closing the window with a bang, she sank down on her haunches and leaned against the hard wall. From the street below came the occasional sound of tires on wet pavement. A faint smell of smoke drifted up from the lantern. Isolated in an island of dim light, she gathered up her legs and rested her chin on her damp knees. Her mind shifted to the past.

How enthralled she had been with Gary, she recalled, a great sadness welling up for her lost innocence.

Ten years older than she, Gary had been a successful businessman with a history that included divorce. It was an unoriginal story. His wife had left him for another man. Secretly, it pleased her that he would share his tormented feelings, and she believed they were forging a bond of trust. He was hurt, yes. But she was certain the strength of her love would make him whole.

How pathetically naive she had been. His emotional wounds were beyond Roseanna's ability to understand, let alone heal. In the end he turned on her, accusing her falsely of his wife's sins. The pain, the humiliation, had felt like knife stabs to her heart.

Roseanna hugged her knees, rocking back and forth in an effort to comfort herself. How could she have been so foolish as to believe her love was strong enough to mend Gary's broken heart? Tears stung her eyes, and she ruthlessly wiped them away. Never again would she set herself up for that kind of suffering.

Her painful memories strengthening her resolve, she decided her feelings for Simon must not be allowed to grow any stronger. The less she saw of him, the less she relied on him, the better. She had to think of a way not to see him again.

But he was coming over the very next morning, she recalled in a flurry of panic. How could she avoid that?

Of course! She would ask Karyn to help. If she could get her friend to come over, the two of them could manage the furniture without his assistance. Filled with purpose, Roseanna pushed herself to her feet and went to phone Karyn.

"Roseanna," she answered at once. "You must be psychic. You're just the person I wanted to talk to." Karyn's voice rang with excitement. "Wait until you see the clothes I bought today. They're fabulous! I got some stuff that looks like my mother would have worn it when she was a teenager. So cool. Then on the way home I stopped to visit my grandmother. She took me up to her attic and showed me a trunk full of old clothes. Shoes and hats included. And they're all in perfect condition! Grandmother used to have a clothing store when she was young, before she had her kids." She stopped only long enough for a breath. "You know how you're always talking about the clothing boutique you'll own someday? Well, I've been thinking along those lines, too, only mine would be funky retro clothes. It would be so incredible."

"It would be great!" Roseanna agreed. She could tell Karyn's mind was a million miles away. She sounded totally obsessed with her idea. At another time Roseanna would have loved discussing it for hours, but right now she had a pressing matter hanging over her. "Karyn, the reason I called is that I need you to come over in the morning and help move some furniture." Roseanna tried to keep the panic out of her voice. "Do you think you could?"

"Oh, sure," Karyn returned in a cheerfully absent tone.

Roseanna sighed with relief. "Thanks. I really need you."

"This is sounding interesting. What's up?"

"I have to get Simon's stuff over to his store." Roseanna offered as short an explanation as she could.

"What about Tim?" Karyn asked.

"He sprained his ankle."

"Too bad."

"Yeah, for him and me. I'm without a helper." Roseanna wanted to know that Karyn would definitely be there tomorrow morning. "You are certain you will come? Early?"

There was a pause. "How early are we talking about?"

"Six-thirty?"

"Oh, man!" Karyn's groan rumbled through the line.

"All right, seven," Roseanna quickly amended. "Don't let me down," she pleaded.

"Hmm," Karyn murmured. "You sound desperate. What's the urgency?"

"I'll tell you later."

"Agreed. See you when the rooster crows."

The following morning Roseanna woke with a start on her living room sofa. She looked around, disoriented. Why wasn't she in bed? She recalled talking to Karyn, having a brief shower, and eating one of the blueberry muffins she had used as a candleholder. Then she had lain on the couch cuddled in her cozy floral comforter to leaf through the fashion magazines by lantern light. Now the periodicals lay scattered on the floor. She must have fallen asleep while reading.

She shot upright. Simon! The windows glowed with the soft light of early morning. She twisted around to look at the clock on the kitchen wall and gasped. Almost 7:30. What had happened to Karyn?

Hurrying to the window, she scanned the courtyard below. The day had dawned clear and cool. At once, her gaze riveted on a familiar tall, dark-haired man heading across the street with long, purposeful strides. Simon!

There was nothing to be done about it. She heaved her window open and watched him as he approached.

"Good morning," she called, clutching her yellow chenille bathrobe to her throat against the nip in the air. Simon crossed the brick courtyard to stand directly below her.

"Good morning yourself," he said, craning upward.

The way he braced his hands on his lean hips caused his jacket to bunch, making his shoulders appear even broader than she remembered. Ruffled by the breeze, his hair looked soft and freshly washed and very appealing. An unwanted tingle of excitement shot through her.

"Give me a few minutes," she said, feeling silly carrying on a conversation with her head out the window. She pulled back her hair, knowing it must look like it did every morning—as though she had danced around a cauldron all night.

"Do you want me to come back?"

"No," she said with a sigh. "You're already here. I'll get dressed and come down."

"Do you have coffee on?"

"I'll make a pot."

"Don't bother. I'll get some for us," he said, turning to leave. "See you in fifteen minutes."

"I need more time!"

He waved and strode off, leaving Roseanna to shut the window with an indignant bang. Simon Oakes resided on earth for the sole purpose of making her life difficult—of that she was certain by now.

Simon returned exactly when he had said he would.

"Breakfast," he announced when she met him at the downstairs door. He held up one of Crab Claw Catering's famous breakfast baskets.

Roseanna barely noticed the offering, her gaze held captive by his. His discerning eyes bore straight to that vulnerable part of her, deep within, that was not sheltered by the armor her memories had forged last night. She prayed he could not see the power he held over her.

"Hello, Roseanna."

"Simon," she whispered, feeling unable to catch her breath. Warmth flooded her cheeks and her heart thumped away like a rock-and-roll band in her chest. She had not underestimated the effect he had on her. She was going to have to be strong. Very strong.

Chapter Five

Simon was married once before, she reminded herself, trying hard to block her interest in him. She refused to risk being hurt again. In order to protect herself she must keep him at arm's length.

Like her, he had dressed for the work, yet he managed to look wildly attractive in a baggy sweatshirt and jeans with a fringed tear in the knee. At the front desk he opened the basket and took out the contents: a thermos, two white china cups, cloth napkins, an assortment of rich pastries, and a pink rose, complete with its own slim glass vase.

Avoiding his gaze and the romantic flower, she poured steaming, aromatic coffee from the thermos. From the assortment of sweeteners she chose turbinado sugar and concentrated on pouring the sparkling amber grains into her coffee.

"This is nice . . . very extravagant," she offered by way of thanks, feeling uncomfortable, yet charmed.

She picked up a plump cheese Danish, her favorite. There was a long moment of silence as they concentrated on their breakfasts. When she at last glanced up, she found him watching her closely.

"You're quiet this morning," he noted.

"I'm just enjoying breakfast."

He didn't look convinced. "Are you sure this is a convenient time?"

"Uh-huh." She lowered her gaze, pretending great interest in stirring cream into her coffee.

Simon did not attempt further conversation. Glancing at him covertly, she noticed his puzzled expression. Guilt and sadness pulled at her. She hated acting so aloof, but what could she do? She had to let him know she did not want to deepen their relationship.

The atmosphere around the desk grew increasingly uncomfortable. Roseanna nibbled at her food, unable to enjoy it. Simon devoured his in a determined way, but she had the feeling he had not tasted a single bite. Frowning, he attacked his sticky fingers with a paper napkin, crumpled it, and tossed it into the wastebasket.

She wiped her own fingers with nervous, finicky dabs. "Shall we get this over with?"

His gaze impaled her. "Roseanna, is everything all right?"

"Of course. I'm just . . . a little preoccupied," she answered lamely. She hadn't intended to give him the cold shoulder, but feared that was what he must be thinking. Calling herself all kinds of an idiot, she hurried off to get the hand truck.

"What do you want to move first?" she asked when she returned to the front of the store where she had grouped his purchases. She was glad to be starting the job. Having a task to focus on made her feel calmer and more in control.

He headed over to the rolltop desk. "Let's tackle the biggest first. Do you have a screwdriver?"

Roseanna went after the wine crate that held her assortment of tools, most of which had been scavenged from the store. Simon sorted through the pitiful jumble until he found what he needed.

Roseanna observed in silent admiration as he disassembled the desk with knowledgeable efficiency. Then they took the first section, the top, across the road and around to the back of his store where there was a large spare room. With their conversation limited to polite requests and brief instructions, they repeated the procedure until everything had been delivered.

As Simon placed the last piece, the filing cabinet, out of the way against a wall, Roseanna glanced around in curiosity. Windows filled the spacious area with light. Furniture in various stages of being reconditioned stood about, but it all somehow looked orderly. The odor of oils and varnishes lingered, not unpleasantly, in the air. Along one wall ran a sturdy workbench on which lay a small art deco lamp that had been taken apart, its glass shade, cord, and brass base all separate. The wall above was covered with pegboard that displayed an amazing variety of tools, putting her wine crate selection to shame.

"I'm impressed," she complimented him. "What a fantastic workplace."

Simon leaned against the workbench, observing her. His intense gaze reminded her of the intimacies they had shared, and her nerves began jumping.

"As long as you're here, why don't you take a look around?" he suggested.

Though the temptation to do so tugged at her, Rose-anna recalled her decision to stay away from him. She cleared her throat. "I, um, really should be getting back."

"Sure," he murmured, his voice flat.

She felt like a heel. Was it really necessary to run away like a scared rabbit? Surely she could manage a casual friendship. "Well, maybe for a few minutes," she gave in.

He rewarded her with a smile, and it amazed her again how easily he could make her feel wonderful. He followed close at her side while she walked through the workshop area, examining with keen interest the tables and chairs and dressers.

"Is this where you recondition furniture before you sell it?" she asked, stopping to admire a pine cabinet.

He nodded. "It's a great feeling to see an abused or neglected item brought back to life."

"I thought that refinishing antique furniture destroyed its value."

"That's true. I only do what is absolutely necessary." He cocked a brow at her. "Where did you learn that?"

"I don't know." She moved about the room, taking everything in. "From Tim, I suppose."

Simon cast a sharp glance her way. "Is he still working for you?"

Roseanna got the distinct impression that Simon didn't like Tim. "He's kind of like a handyman. He just comes when I need something done, and he minds the store for me occasionally, too. I'm lucky I have someone like him to depend on."

"From now on if you need help call me."

"Thanks. I'll remember that. But I wouldn't want to impose. With Tim it's simply a part-time job. Since I pay him, I never need to worry that I'm taking advantage of a friendship."

"Doesn't he have other work?"

"No. He's going to school, getting a degree in fine arts. He's very talented." She ran a hand along the surface of a polished desk, its golden patina reminding her of the color of Simon's eyes. "He painted the sign outside my shop."

Simon didn't say any more, but his expression remained sober. He had never said anything against Tim, but Roseanna sensed something amiss.

Examining a china hutch with a broken pane of glass, she decided to change the subject. "How do you know so much about antiques?"

"Collecting and restoring them has been my hobby for years." He cracked a smile. "The hours I spend refinishing or repairing furniture helps keep me sane. You've probably seen the light on over here at night."

She had seen his van and the glow from the back of the building on several occasions. Despite her mixed feelings about Simon, it was comforting to think of him being so nearby in the evenings.

"Come and see the main showroom." He nodded for her to follow him. "I've been wanting to show you around."

"I have to confess, I've peeked in the front windows. Checking out the competition, you know."

"What did you think?"

The serious tone of his question flattered her. "I was impressed," she answered with sincerity.

A look of pride spread across his face. Seeing how much Simon loved his work, she felt a bit envious. After all, it was also her greatest desire to own a business she could put her whole heart into. Running a secondhand store wasn't as bad as she had first thought it would be, and sometimes it was even fun and exciting, but her dream of someday being the proprietor of a clothing boutique still tugged at her.

He led her into the showroom. Although the store was not as big as hers it appeared spacious because of the lack of clutter and limited amount of merchandise. The high-quality antiques he offered for sale had been arranged in intimate, room-like groupings. She went over to a desk, rug, and lamp combination she thought was particularly attractive.

"It's clever the way you placed the fountain pen and beautiful writing paper on the desk." She fingered the colorful, leaded-glass lamp, admiring it. "You made it look as though someone could sit down and begin composing a letter. I can imagine this entire grouping in someone's home."

"That was exactly what I had in mind."

Next she moved to a bedroom set. He had made it up with a wedding ring quilt and mound of soft pillows. A slim crystal vase with a delicate bouquet of pink roses and baby's breath graced the nightstand, along with a leather-bound copy of *Lady Chatterly's Lover.* The setting looked like it had come straight out of a home decor magazine.

"This is really beautiful," she offered with genuine enthusiasm.

"Thank you," he returned simply, looking very pleased. "I can't wait to see what you intend to do with your place."

Roseanna shrugged. "To tell you the truth, I hadn't made any plans beyond cleaning and organizing."

"I have a feeling that will change."

The front door's brass bell chimed, announcing the arrival of a tall, trim man with thick silver hair. He wore a pair of striped overalls with a denim shirt and held a foil-covered plate.

"Don't let me keep you from your business," she whispered.

"That's not a customer." He grinned. "That's my father."

Simon introduced them. From his warm and open demeanor, Roseanna could tell Simon enjoyed a good relationship with his dad. As for herself, she liked Mr. Oakes instantly. His handshake was firm and respectful, and his smile sincere. It was obvious where Simon had gotten his twinkling amber eyes.

"It's nice to meet you, Mr. Oakes."

"Please, we're neighbors. Call me Andrew."

"I don't know what I would have done without Dad," Simon told her. "He's been here every day since

I signed the lease, working nonstop to get the store put together."

"You did a great job," she said to the older man. "This place is wonderful."

Andrew shrugged. "I can't take the credit. I just followed Simon's orders. He has his own style, his own way of doing things."

"You're exaggerating, Dad," Simon refuted. "You had some terrific suggestions."

Roseanna noticed Andrew watching her with keen interest and supposed he was wondering about her relationship with Simon.

"Do your folks help you out at your place?" Andrew asked.

"My dad passed away when I was very little, and my mother never remarried. She lives about an hour away, but she works full time and is awfully busy. I have a hired man I use occasionally."

Andrew pulled the foil off the plate and offered her a cookie. "Oatmeal. Help yourself."

She took two plump, raisin-studded cookies. "My favorite, thanks."

He gave her a good-natured wink. "Well, if you ever need anything, and can't get this brute over to help, you just call me."

As her confused feelings about Simon resurfaced, Roseanna felt her cheeks begin to heat. "I'll do that," she mumbled, looking down at her watch. "It's nearly nine o'clock. I had better head over to my place and open up."

Simon walked her to the front door. "Give me a call

some time," he suggested, leaning against the door-jamb with his muscular arms crossed.

Smiling to avoid a reply, Roseanna gave him a merry little wave and fled.

Roseanna was heading for the back of her building when she heard the bell she had just finished installing over the front door. She had liked Simon's and didn't mind copying a good idea. Karyn entered, carrying a large paper bag.

"Hi," Roseanna called out. "I'm back here." When Karyn joined her, Roseanna pointed toward the basement stairs. "Want to see the dungeon? I was just going down."

"Sure. I'll turn your sign to CLOSED."

Roseanna looked at her watch and was surprised to find it was half past five. Her visit to Simon's shop that morning had energized her and renewed her enthusiasm for her own store. He seemed to think she had the ability to create something wonderful. She didn't know about that, but there really was a lot more she could do here.

Karyn joined her and together they descended the back staircase. "Sorry I didn't show up this morning," she apologized. "Another girl called in sick, and so I had to go into work early."

"That's okay. It worked out all right."

Roseanna found what she was looking for—the wine crate of old tools. As she dug through them she recalled with envy Simon's well-laid-out back room and decided it was time to purchase some decent supplies, a container to store them . . . and maybe a work-bench, too.

"This is spooky down here. A good place for ghosts to hang out," Karyn said as she gazed around with a grimace. In a chartreuse bell-bottom jumpsuit and thick-soled shoes, another of her retro outfits, she created a brilliant spot of color in the gloomy surroundings.

"Ugh! Don't even mention ghosts. Sometimes at night I think I hear noises downstairs in the shop. It's creepy."

Karyn gave her a comforting smile. "I was just kidding. This old building is probably a mouse motel. Get a cat."

"Yeah, that's what Tim says, too. Maybe I will." Finding the tool she needed, Roseanna went over to tighten the screws on a captain's chair. The repair only took a few minutes, and now the item was ready to be put out for sale. She smiled to herself in satisfaction. Simon would be proud of her.

Karyn watched the whole proceeding with interest. "You're becoming quite the handywoman. Is someone inspiring you?" she asked with a hint of coyness in her voice.

"I just want to get this place fixed up better," Roseanna hedged.

"Ambitious women have big appetites. It's a good thing I brought dinner."

Roseanna thought of Simon's breakfast basket and his father's cookies. This was the third time that day someone was feeding her, she mused, her stomach rumbling. "You are a life saver. Let's eat over here."

Motioning toward a 1950s-style table, she brought over the chair she had just repaired and joined Karyn.

Above them hung a barroom light made out of bright plastic, a large crack marring one side. Broken furniture and dilapidated cardboard boxes filled with who-knew-what-all lined the walls. Roseanna had yet to muster the heart or energy to sort through the mess.

Karyn glanced around. "This basement would be a great place for a Halloween party—but not much else. Why don't you clean it out and use it for store space?"

"Maybe I will someday . . . if I keep Treasures that long." Roseanna removed the wrapping from the hefty hoagie-style sandwich and immediately tucked into it.

Karyn's gaze focused on Roseanna's neck. "What's that?" She leaned across the table to touch the emerald necklace. "Wow!"

Roseanna's fingers flew to the jewelry she had impulsively put on when she had returned from Simon's that morning.

"Where did you get it?" Karyn asked.

"It was my great-aunt's," Roseanna explained, going on to tell the story of how Simon discovered the treasure hidden in the watchmaker's cabinet.

Karyn looked around with renewed interest. "You mean to tell me that your aunt might have more things stashed?"

Roseanna shrugged. "I wouldn't be surprised. The older she got the stranger her habits became. Once I overheard her having an argument with my mother about not putting her money in the bank. I guess she was squirreling that away, too."

"Have you found any?"

"Not yet, unfortunately."

"If I were you I'd be tearing the walls apart."

Roseanna laughed. "I'm sure my landlord would like that."

As they ate in companionable silence, Roseanna's thoughts strayed to the night Simon had returned the necklace. That led to the recollection of the kiss they had shared, in vivid, luscious, tingling detail. And then of the ride to the coffee shop when she had learned of his divorce.

Roseanna noticed Karyn watching her thoughtfully.

Karyn put down her sandwich. "Something's bothering you."

"No, I've been thinking about what to do with the shop."

Karyn was not about to be put off so easily. "It's written all over your face."

In an attempt to avoid Karyn's discerning gaze, Roseanna carefully rearranged the tomatoes on her sandwich. "You're seeing things that aren't there."

Undaunted by Roseanna's denial, Karyn continued doggedly, "You don't have to tell me if you don't want to . . . but I'll bet a month's hors d'oeuvres the problem is tall, brown-haired, and has a very nice antiques store right across the street."

It took an effort not to squirm in her seat. Simon drew her in a powerful way, yet Roseanna had no intention of following her feelings.

"Maybe."

"Maybe, nothing," Karyn mocked. She popped open her can of cream soda and sat back, eyeing Roseanna with amusement.

"You're infuriating sometimes, you know that?"

Karyn just shrugged, an impish gleam in her eyes. "You're devouring that sandwich like you're starved. Have you had anything to eat since the pastries?"

That caught Roseanna's attention. "Pastries?"

"In the breakfast basket," Karyn said slowly, as though savoring the moment. "Boy, was I surprised to see your friendly neighborhood antiques dealer walk through the door. He ordered the basket and didn't say where he was going with it, but it wasn't hard to guess." She arched a brow, a smug look plastered on her face. "By the way, I was the one who suggested your favorite, cheese Danish."

Roseanna's throat tightened. Suddenly she regretted having confided in Karyn about her dates with Simon. Of course, they had not really been dates. Dates were prearranged events, not the spontaneous encounters she'd had with Simon. They had been . . . what? She chewed her lip, annoyed she couldn't find an adequate way to describe the time she had spent with him.

"You might as well get that gleam out of your eyes. I'm not interested in him."

Karyn's mouth pursed. Instead of putting her off, Roseanna's denial seemed to intrigue her friend. "Roseanna," she drawled. "You are so transparent. Now, you said his name is Simon Oakes, correct? I like that. Distinguished. And he is pretty incredible to look at, too."

"Oh, all right," Roseanna grumbled. "Let me re-phrase. I refuse to be interested." Her heart had already suffered a deep wound, and if any man had the ability

to do that fragile organ in for good, it was Simon
Oakes.

"What's the problem?"

"He's divorced."

Karyn nodded her head, tsk-tsking in a solemn fashion. "A divorced man. What scum. He should have a
big red *D* stamped on his forehead as a warning to all
women."

Roseanna sighed. "I'm serious."

"So am I."

The compassion in Karyn's expression told Roseanna she sincerely wanted to help. But that was an
impossible task. The situation was hopeless.

"What Gary did to you was wrong," Karyn continued, her tone serious now. "He obviously possessed
less character than overcooked zucchini. But why put
all divorced men in his category?"

"Because a secondhand man is damaged goods."

Karyn shook her head, not buying it. "Everybody
has trouble in their life. They get past it."

"Some do."

"Most do."

"Oh, you're probably right," Roseanna snapped, re-
acting with an irrational flare of temper. Immediately
sorry for her outburst, she took a calming breath before she went on. "Nevertheless, I loved Gary, and his
lack of trust devastated me. You probably wouldn't
understand unless it had happened to you." Talking
about it brought a dull ache to the region of her heart.
She had gotten over Gary and yet the emotional scar
remained. "I suppose the real problem is that I can't
tell who's going to be okay and who isn't. I can't trust

my own judgment." She twined her hands together and studied them, grieved by her admission. "Gary cared for me. I do think that he did, in some meaningful way. I must have been blind, not seeing I was just a rebound relationship."

"I do understand," Karyn insisted kindly. "Nevertheless, don't you think you're being a little unfair to yourself . . . and to Simon? How can you be so sure he's not a good man, an honorable man? You're refusing to even give him a chance."

Roseanna's clamped jaw must have revealed her stubborn mind-set, for Karyn smiled in a resigned way and let the uncomfortable subject drop. She fished into the bag she had brought and placed a handful of macadamia and white chocolate chunk cookies on the table. Sharing was a way of life for Karyn and was the characteristic Roseanna loved most in her friend. Whether it was food or the intimate details of her life, Karyn did not hesitate to give.

"You might as well know the worst of it," Roseanna mumbled, toying with a cookie. "Simon and I, um, kissed. More than once."

"I knew it," Karyn declared, eyes flashing. "When I saw Simon this morning I had a strong feeling something was happening between you two."

"That's what I'm so scared about," Roseanna whimpered, overwhelmed by her tumultuous emotions. Unable to sit still, she shoved her chair back and began pacing. "I don't want to take a chance. I've always thought of myself as someone who learns from her mistakes. I'd be an utter fool to put myself in a position to get hurt again."

"On the other hand, you might be a bigger fool if you let your fears rule your life." Karyn crumpled her sandwich wrapping. "End of lecture."

"I'm so mixed up," Roseanna admitted. "What should I do?"

"That's simple," Karyn said. "Just follow your heart."

"That will be thirty dollars." Smiling brightly, Roseanna wrapped the three delicate china cups and matching saucers carefully and handed them to Karyn's grandmother.

Karyn joined them at the front desk. "I've been telling Gram what a great place you have."

"Oh, I do like this store. It is so charming," Mrs. Hartly praised. "I had a shop, too, when I was your age. Not like this, though."

"I know. It was a clothing store." Roseanna slipped her check into the register. "Karyn told me. Someday I'd like a clothing boutique."

"I really enjoyed it. Kept it until the kids started coming along." She sighed, her ample chest heaving a bit from the effort. "Nearly broke my heart to have to let it go." Her forlorn expression lasted only a moment. "But that's all in the past now. Be grateful for what you have, Roseanna. This shop is *your* treasure."

Karyn let her grandmother amble out the door first. "How's it going with you-know-who?" she whispered.

Roseanna refused to meet her friend's penetrating gaze. It had been two weeks since their heart-to-heart talk in the basement. "It's not."

"You might be making a big mistake."

"Or I might be saving myself a big heartache."

After Karyn had gone, Roseanna wandered aimlessly through the store, her friend's well-meant advice bothering her. Her last customers were two middle-aged women with determined mouths who were scanning a sale table laden with chipped Fiestaware, stray demitasse cups, old kitchen appliances, and a shoe box full of faded postcards.

After she rang up their few small purchases, she followed them to the doors to lock up. As she was turning her sign to CLOSED she saw Simon doing the same. He caught her gaze and waved. Her heart in her throat, she returned the friendly gesture. Simon disappeared inside his shop.

Roseanna went over to her cash register, took out the money and checks from that day's sales, then had to tally the amount three times before she was certain she had done it right. She couldn't concentrate.

What should she do? She asked herself the question for the hundredth time. Should she, as Karyn suggested, follow her heart? That seemed the easy way—but it was full of peril. Even considering it aroused awful sensations of anxiety. While Karyn had made some valid points, Roseanna didn't think herself wrong, either.

She reached into a drawer to retrieve her purse and saw the antique pricing book Simon had brought over for her. That had been a very thoughtful gesture and she had appreciated it. He seemed like such a good man.

Unable to endure one more second of waffling, Roseanna forced herself to come to a decision. Before she lost her nerve, she dialed the phone. As she waited for an answer her pulse raced wildly. When Simon's deep voice came across the line, her heart skipped a beat and began hammering in her chest. Trying not to sound as nervous as she felt, she invited him over.

He sounded surprised, then cautious as he answered, "Sure. I'm just about finished up with a project. I'll be a few minutes."

"Well, if you're busy—"

"No, no. I'm coming."

"Okay." She tried to think of something else to say, but was at a loss.

She hung up feeling as silly and giddy as a teenager asking the cutest boy in class for a date. She sank back into the cozy comfort of her big leather desk chair and hugged her arms about herself.

This was it—she was about to play with fire. She would give Simon a chance.

Chapter Six

"That must have been an interesting phone call," Andrew Oakes commented. He sat on a stool at the workbench where he was busy repairing the wobbly legs on a small stool.

Simon shrugged nonchalantly.

"Must have been that young lady." Andrew chuckled. "Your expression gave you away. I can always tell when something is happening with you."

Simon ignored him, playing it cool. His father was a meddler. To make it worse, the older he got the more entitled he felt to pry into Simon's personal affairs. It made no difference that Andrew's opinions and judgments nearly always turned out to be right. Simon didn't like being told what to do any more now than he had when he was ten, and they'd had numerous good-natured quarrels about this less-than-endearing characteristic. Nothing Simon said seemed to have any long-term effect. Andrew was unrepentant.

Avoiding his father's discerning eyes, Simon turned his back and bent over the shop's deep-welled concrete sink to clean the brush he had just used to varnish a table. Turpentine fumes filled the air.

"I've got to install an exhaust fan in here."

"That *was* Roseanna, wasn't it?" Andrew persisted.

Simon gritted his teeth. "Yep."

"I liked her. She's nice, don't you think?"

Simon kept his voice neutral. "I wouldn't know." He began to whistle, pretending vast disinterest in the subject of their conversation.

"I'll just bet you know a whole lot more than you're letting on."

Simon frowned to himself. "You have an active imagination, Dad."

His father chuckled. "Well now, I suppose that's true enough. But it doesn't take much imagination to see what was going on between you and that red-headed gal. When she was here there was enough electricity in this place to cause a power surge."

His father's observations stirred up the emotions Simon had been struggling to keep in check since he had last seen Roseanna. "Don't jump to conclusions," he responded more tersely than he had intended. Scolding himself for the slipup, he continued to scrub his brush vigorously.

"Touchy on this subject?"

"No," Simon muttered.

"You been seeing her?"

"No."

"Hmph. That's a shame."

It was a good thing his dad had decided not to go on, for Simon had had just about all of that topic he could handle. He didn't want to discuss Roseanna. Not when he felt at such a loss figuring out what was happening between them.

Since his divorce, Simon had not been remotely interested in women, and had prided himself on being sensible. But ever since he had laid eyes on Roseanna, his emotions had taken him on a roller coaster ride. It was all so unexpected that he had been left reeling and bewildered.

When he'd last seen Roseanna, the morning they'd brought over his things two weeks before, he had gotten the distinct impression that she was giving him the brush-off.

He had tried to tell himself he didn't care, but that was darned hard to do when Roseanna refused to leave his thoughts. Often he'd glance across the street to see if he might catch a glimpse of her, only to become angry with himself for acting like such a fool.

Simon finished rinsing his brush and hung it to dry. He realized he was glowering when he looked up to find his father eyeing him in a considering manner.

"I understand the divorce was a blow to you," Andrew remarked, his tone gruff and matter-of-fact. "You and Janelle vowed to love each other and stay together. That you couldn't work out your differences is a tragedy." He paused as though waiting for that to sink in. "Still, life is a learning process. If we're lucky we get a second chance."

"Thanks for the advice, Dad," Simon replied insincerely. He quickly washed his hands, rolled down his sleeves, then reached for his jacket.

Andrew set the stool onto the floor and stepped on it to test it. "Solid." He pursed his lips. "If only the human heart could be mended so easily."

Simon rolled his eyes as he headed toward the door. "I have to go out for a while."

"Wait." His dad reached for the package he had brought into the store. "Give these to Roseanna. That is where you're going, isn't it?"

Simon gave his dad a wry look. "All right, I give up. Yes, I'm going over to see her. But please don't go getting any wild ideas. There is nothing between us except the street."

Andrew held up his age-worn hands in mock defense. "Okay. But I'm warning you, if you don't ask her over for dinner soon, *I* intend to."

Roseanna scurried around the store, straightening furniture that didn't need to be straightened, and dusting what didn't need to be dusted. The anticipation of seeing Simon again had turned her into a nervous cyclone of energy, and she was practically perched on top of an armoire, straining to remove cobwebs, when she heard her doorbell tinkling. He had arrived.

She scrambled down, dropping her spray bottle of lemon-scented furniture polish in her haste. "Hi," she said, her voice emerging in a shy, squeaky tone that was so revealing she felt her face turn red.

"Hi, yourself," he responded warmly, retrieving the polish and handing it to her. "It's nice to finally see you again."

The sincerity in his tone warmed her heart. He sounded like he had truly missed her. "I've been busy."

He looked good in trim jeans, button-down shirt, and leather jacket. The smell of varnish that clung to him made it obvious he had been busy in his beloved shop again. Roseanna liked it that he worked with his hands and wasn't afraid to get dirty when necessary.

He handed her a brown paper package. "Compliments of my dad."

Roseanna quickly set her cleaning supplies aside and opened his gift, discovering a mound of chocolate-chip cookies. She immediately snatched one up and took a bite. "Oh, my favorite," she said around the mouthful.

Simon took one, too, and devoured it in two bites. "I thought oatmeal was your favorite."

"They both are. Your father is an angel."

Bracing his hands on his hips, Simon made a thorough visual sweep of the room. "Wow. You weren't kidding. You really have been busy."

Infused with a warm glow of pride from his compliment, Roseanna met his amber eyes. But when she saw they brimmed with questions, intimate questions she wasn't yet prepared to answer, she quickly looked away.

She had decided to take a risk on Simon, and she would. That didn't mean she had forgotten her previous bad experience. She intended to take things slowly and carefully.

"I was so impressed with your store that I copied your idea of room groupings. That's why I called. I wanted to show you." She couldn't help sprouting a self-satisfied grin as she walked over to the first setting. "Mine could never be elegant like yours are, so I went in another direction. Funky."

Roseanna presented her first arrangement, a green canvas hammock stretched on a metal frame on which lay a battered travel guide to the Bahamas, a hot pink beach towel, a pair of rhinestone-encrusted sunglasses, and a bottle of super-strength sunscreen. On the floor beneath she had created a small sand pile in which were stuck a pair of flip-flops.

"I could lie right down and pretend I was in Nassau," Simon remarked as he set the hammock to swinging.

"You ain't seen nothin' yet," she said, her excitement bubbling to the surface. "Look up there." She pointed to the huge stuffed marlin she'd dragged out of the basement and had Tim help her mount on the wall.

Simon stepped closer, and again chuckled. "There's a toy fisherman dangling out of its mouth."

"I call it 'The fish's revenge.' "

Next, Roseanna showed him a child-sized iron bed with chipped white paint, now layered with clean old blankets in various colors and patterns. The pillows, sham, and skirt were matching white with crisply starched lace trim. On the bed sat three aging Teddy bears next to the children's book, *The Three Bears.*

"The last one is my favorite," Roseanna told him, leading him across the store to the small side room that she hoped would not leak anymore since she had insisted her landlord have it repaired. There she presented her last and best effort. "This is the seventies room."

She pushed aside the beaded doorway to allow Simon inside. The odor of sandalwood incense greeted them. Covering the floor was an orange shag rug. Plants growing out of terra-cotta containers abounded, some on the floor and some held in macramé hangers. Posters of Janis Joplin, the Grateful Dead, and intricate psychedelic designs filled the walls. Next to a matching Papassan sofa and chair set was an Indian brass table with several candles and a book entitled *The Hitchhiker's Guide to America.* Simon nodded to the record player with three-foot-high speakers that sat on the floor over in a corner.

"My parents had a stereo like that when I was a teenager. Boy, does that bring back memories." He inspected the equipment. "This is a beauty. I'll bet it was expensive when it was new."

Roseanna cocked her head. "Do you want to play something?"

"Do I get to pick?"

"Sure."

Together they sat cross-legged on the rug in front of the old record player. Roseanna watched as Simon flipped through the stack of albums, often exclaiming or laughing in recognition.

With a crackling noise, the needle found the beginning groove on the record and soon the energetic sounds of a Beatles tune filled the room.

Simon rose to his feet and switched off the overhead light to submerge the space in semi-darkness, with only the borrowed glow from the main store lights to see by. Before Roseanna had a chance to protest, he lit the candles with a matchbook he'd found nearby. He returned to recline next to her, lying on his side.

Roseanna leaned back, bracing herself with her palms on the fuzzy rug. His presence filled the space, crowding against her, and the mood inside the small space was intoxicating.

"This is just the beginning," she told him, trying to keep her mind on anything but how giddy she was feeling. "I have a lot more ideas."

"Maybe you should have a supply of miniskirts and bell-bottoms and beads," he suggested.

"You must be thinking of my friend, Karyn. She's the one into retro clothing. I never know what crazy outfit I'll see her in next."

"That style is popular right now. Old clothing can sell for an amazing amount of money." He pursed his lips, his expression thoughtful. "Say, I've just had an idea. If your friend has a passion for old clothes and is knowledgeable about them, why don't you have her help you set up a clothing area? You could pay her a consulting fee."

Roseanna considered it. "I've seen whole stores specializing in vintage clothing. And I do have plenty of space downstairs, even to build dressing rooms." She suddenly sat up straighter. "Guess what I have in the basement?"

"Besides spiders?"

"Mannequins! I'd forgotten about them until just now. Aunt Tildy had bought all the fixtures and display cases and other things from a store going out of business."

"With what you've already got going you could begin to advertise with a different slant. You don't have *used* merchandise anymore." His eyes widened. "Now you sell vintage nostalgia. Very 'in.' "

"That's a great idea! I'm going to give this some thought." She looked around the room, enjoying Simon's enthusiasm and feeling immensely pleased with herself. "You know what?"

"What?"

"This is starting to be fun. This store, I mean. What a revelation."

"Are you starting to like the secondhand business?"

"Like it?" The notion shocked her. For a long moment she turned the thought over in her mind. "Let's say I don't dislike it anymore."

For several minutes they listened to the music without talking, each lost in their own thought. Roseanna stared into the yellow flickering light of the candles. The atmosphere she had created in the small room made it seem separated from the real world; it was their own private world. She wished that time would stand still.

But then the record came to an end, abruptly breaking the spell. She looked over at Simon and discovered him gazing at her. With a gentle smile he reached up and brushed a strand of hair from her cheek. Roseanna's breath caught in her throat. How easy it would be to lean a little closer and snuggle against him.

Worried about how things might progress if they stayed there much longer, Roseanna forced herself to get up and turn on the lights. Simon switched off the stereo, leaned over to blow out the candles, and with a sigh rose to his feet.

Roseanna led the way back to the front desk, where she reached for another cookie. "I can't resist."

"My dad loves to cook and feed people." Simon eyed Roseanna. "As a matter of fact, he told me that I'd better invite you over for dinner soon or he would beat me to the punch. You made quite a splash with him."

"I liked your dad, too. Tell him I'd enjoy having dinner with him."

"I think I will," he said with a sudden, determined air. Joining her where she leaned against the desk, he reached for the phone. "May I?"

"Of course." Puzzled, Roseanna watched him punch out a number, the way the corner of his mouth crooked upward causing alarm bells to peal in her head. "What are you doing?"

He winked at her as he spoke into the phone. "Hello, Dad. Guess what? Roseanna's coming to dinner." He glanced over at her and grinned. "How's tonight?"

"Simon, I didn't mean—"

He cut off her protest, asking, "Do you have plans?"

"Not exactly."

"She says she's free as a bird," Simon quipped into the phone.

"Simon!"

He wasn't paying attention to her. He nodded his head while listening to the phone. Then he caught Roseanna's eye. "Dad wants to know if clam chowder is all right with you. That's his specialty.

"S-sure," she sputtered.

"She says she loves it." While he talked with his father his twinkling eyes never left her. "Seven." He raised his brows at her and she shrugged, reaching for another cookie. He grabbed her hand and whispered, "Don't ruin your appetite." Into the phone he said, "Great. We'll bring the wine." Without releasing his grip, he replaced the telephone receiver.

Roseanna didn't know what to say. So much for her plan to go slowly. Being with Simon was like stepping onto a speeding train—thrilling, exhilarating, but it made her feel so out of control!

"I need to change," she mumbled.

"I'm going to head home. I'll be back to pick you up in half an hour."

"This chowder is delicious," Roseanna told Simon's father, sincere in her enthusiasm as she scooped up another spoonful. "And the table is lovely," she added, surprised and touched at how much trouble he had gone to. A fresh bouquet of yellow tulips and a pair of white candles in crystal holders graced the center of the round linen-draped table. "You went to a lot of trouble."

"Not at all," Andrew returned. Casually elegant in dark slacks and a burgundy turtleneck sweater, he looked like a different man. "It's been long time since I had a beautiful woman to dine with." His face fell ever so slightly. "You see, Simon's mother died several years ago."

"I'm sorry to hear that," Roseanna said.

Simon smiled warmly at his father. "I thought you

were seeing . . . what was her name? Oh, yes, Libby. The one you met at the exercise club. I noticed you were suddenly very interested in working out."

Andrew cleared his throat. "That's for my health." He glanced at Roseanna. "I had a heart attack last year."

"I'm sorry to hear that," Roseanna said.

"Don't be. It changed my life," he returned with a wink. "But that's another story. What I would really like is to hear about you."

"I don't know what to say," Roseanna tried to put him off, feeling self-conscious.

Simon patted her hand. "You might as well start when you were in diapers and tell him everything. He'll get it out of you eventually, anyway."

"Simon," his father protested. "You're scaring the girl."

"I was only stating a fact."

"Hmph." Ignoring Simon, he treated Roseanna to a disarming smile. "That old place you've got is a gem. Simon mentioned that you inherited it. . . ."

Roseanna found herself deep in conversation with Andrew through most of the meal, with Simon seemingly content to listen and observe. Andrew, she realized as she prattled on, had a way with people. From the image she had gotten of Simon's father in his overalls, she had imagined him as a sweet, simple, hardworking man. But the instant Simon pulled into the driveway of his father's elegant house, perched on a hillside overlooking the Chesapeake Bay, Roseanna knew she had drawn the wrong conclusions. There was obviously more to Simon's father than she had first thought.

Simon, too, was showing his other side tonight. In tailored cream trousers, an ivory shirt with pale brown stripes, and dark brown sport jacket, he reminded her of the intimidating man she met the morning of her sale.

Since she had gotten to know him, she realized there was nothing about him to be afraid of. He did possess a strong personality that sometimes overwhelmed her and a keen wit she occasionally struggled to meet head on, yet she had come to know that inside he was a good and gentle man, with values matching her own. The feelings he aroused now sparked a very different kind of concern.

All he needed to do was to look at her, as he was doing at this very moment with his gaze seeming to bore right into her secret thoughts, to cause her to flush and tremble.

In a graceful motion, Simon's father pushed back his chair and rose to his feet.

"I'll help clear," Roseanna said and started to rise, eager to get away from Simon for a moment.

Andrew waved her back down. "Don't get up, dear. Simon will get coffee. I'll return in a while with dessert."

Roseanna sank into her seat, defeated. In a few minutes, Simon returned from the kitchen alone with a gorgeous silver coffee service.

"I'm starting to feel spoiled," she said, looking up at him with a smile. "I'll give you about two hours to stop this treatment."

"I'll see what I can do." Simon filled her china cup and one for himself, moved his chair closer, and sat down. "Dad is busy concocting something. He said to tell you he would be a while."

"Oh, I see. He's giving us time alone."

"You are correct." He nodded solemnly. "And I, for one, intend to thoroughly enjoy it."

The atmosphere became very intimate, very quickly, causing Roseanna to fidget in her Queen Anne chair. She had worn her hair up and when Simon draped his arm behind her and began to caress the back of her neck she rose abruptly to her feet.

"Why don't you show me the view," she rushed. "The deck looks so inviting."

"That's a good idea." Taking her hand as if it were the most natural thing in the world to do, he led her through the French doors onto a spacious porch. Passing up the Adirondack-style chairs, they went over to lean against the waist-high railing. It was a perfectly clear night with the stars putting on a dazzling show and a full moon making it bright enough to see the boats moored at the dock below. Breathing in the cool air and listening to the pleasant clanging sound of halyards hitting masts, she felt herself relaxing enough to absorb all the magic of the moment.

Simon released her hand so that he could drape his jacket over her shoulders, and then slipped his arm beneath the coat and around her waist. It was a simple, comforting gesture with no suggestion that it might lead to anything else. Feeling more at ease, she snuggled against him.

"Did you grow up in this beautiful home?" she asked.

"Yes."

Roseanna detected a hint of sadness in his voice and wondered about it. "It must have been nice."

"Sometimes," he hedged. "Things were different for you as a child, weren't they?"

"I'll say. Our whole house could have fit inside your living room. My sisters and I shared a tiny bedroom. My poor brother had to sleep on the lumpy hide-a-bed in the living room."

"You said you were poor. What was that like for you?"

"We never did have much money. Then Dad died in a hunting accident when I was just nine, leaving us even worse off."

Remembering the death of her father and the difficult times that ensued brought a wave of sadness. Simon must have sensed her discomfort because he drew her even closer.

"Go on," he urged gently.

It became suddenly important for Simon to understand her. "Mom went to work, but her job at the feed and grain store hardly paid the bills."

"It sounds like times were tough."

"Very. And it affected us all in different ways. Right after high school, my sister, Christie, fell in love and got married. All she'd ever dreamed of was to be a wife and stay-at-home mom. She was a Martha Stewart in the making. She wanted to give her children the wonderful, fantasy childhood she'd felt she had missed out on. But the marriage failed, and now her three little kids are in daycare while she struggles to make ends meet.

"Evelyn, the beauty in the family, yearned to be a model." Roseanna laughed at the memory. "We would tease her about spending so much time in front of the mirror posing and primping. Being poor, Evelyn felt like a nobody."

"Is she someone famous now?" Simon asked.

"No. We all encouraged her, but in the end she lacked the confidence to go for it. Now she sells cosmetics in an expensive Washington, D.C. store and is dating an ambitious young politician."

"Maybe she'll be the first lady someday."

"Yes, but not president." She wrinkled her nose at Simon. "Do you understand?"

"She doesn't believe in herself."

"Lastly, I remember my brother, Darren, the oldest of us, always drawing. Boy, would he ever brag about how he was going to be a great architect someday. And he did have a gift. Yet he let it go, too. The older he got the less he drew until he just stopped altogether. He joined the Air Force. I think he did that because he had to shoulder so much responsibility after Dad died. He probably thought his drawing was a foolish pastime to be put aside when he was a man. Growing up having so little, always worried about money, he feared not having a secure job. I suppose he thought joining the service was more practical than chasing a childhood dream."

"What about you?" Simon asked, his dark, probing gaze and caring tone encouraging her to continue.

"I didn't want to let my dreams disappear like they

did." She raised a hand and squeezed her fingers into a fist. "I wanted to hold on tight and not lose heart and not be afraid. When I graduated high school I was determined to be the first in our family to go to college. I wanted more than anything to study business and someday own a clothing boutique. I helped out at Aunt Tildy's secondhand store every summer through high school to save money."

"What happened?"

"I got derailed, too, I guess," she answered, unable to keep the pain from her voice. Her heart ached as she thought about the time when life had still seemed so full of promise. Her first real job after high school graduation had been at a trendy clothing store, and she had loved it. She had put away every penny for college, determined to get her business degree. Owning a clothing store had felt like a very reachable goal.

Then she had met Gary . . . and had foolishly spent all of her savings on a wedding that was not to be. Her heart had turned her into an fool and destroyed her dreams.

"Do you want to tell me more about it?" Simon asked gently.

She shook her head quickly then turned her attention upward to study the glittering stars, giving the gentle night breeze time to cool her face and her emotions. Simon held her close, and she felt her heart squeeze with the most incredibly tender feelings. This was one of those moments in life she would always remember. Refusing to let it be spoiled, she calmed her mind and let the disturbing thoughts dissolve into the darkness. In a mere second, she felt at peace again.

The pain had simply vanished, instantly and completely. Her heart felt as fresh and vulnerable as it had when she was a child.

Simon seemed to understand. "No, not tonight . . . some other time. Tell me about your dreams instead." He wove his fingers between hers and squeezed. "Still holding on tight?"

She smiled up at him. "Yes, I think I am, even though life has given me some twists and turns."

"Like inheriting a secondhand store?"

"Exactly," she said, feeling light and brave. "I'm very glad to have it, of course, but I didn't know what to do with it at first. Truthfully, I was horrified. Me, own a secondhand store!" Remembering her reaction at the time, she could hardly believe it. It seemed so humorous now. Her feelings for the store had changed so much since then. "At first I didn't know what to do with the place. I thought about just selling all the merchandise I could and closing up. Then I realized that if I could make it into a thriving business I might then be able to sell it for a tidy sum. I would then be a lot closer to opening the clothing boutique I really want."

"Has having a clothing store always been your goal?"

"I guess it doesn't sound very important," she answered, feeling self-conscious. "But yes, that's it. Let me try to explain. You see, I grew up wearing hand-me-downs from my two older sisters—or worse, used clothes from Aunt Tildy's shop. I longed for pretty things to wear, clothes that were new and expensive." She halted and wrinked her nose. "Do you want to hear the worst thing that ever happened at school?"

"Who did that to you?" Simon gave her a mock furious look. "I'll have them wiped out."

"Thanks. That would be Missy Calhoun," Roseanna told him, grinning. His jesting kept the atmosphere light, and she was grateful. "When I was fourteen a boy I really liked invited me to a school dance, and I had nothing to wear. Aunt Tildy came to the rescue with a party dress she had in the secondhand store. I knew it came from the shop but it was so beautiful that I pretended it was new. I wore it to a school dance, feeling like a princess."

Simon shook his head. "Uh-oh. I smell trouble brewing."

"Oh, yes," Roseanna replied, nodding grimly. "That dress had belonged to Missy Calhoun, a girl in my class . . . of course, the girl who I didn't get along with. When she saw me at the dance in her discarded dress she burst out laughing. Then she and a bunch of her snooty friends started pointing at me and chanting Secondhand Rose, Secondhand Rose, holes in her hose' right in front of the boy. I was so humiliated that I ran out of the gymnasium and a mile home through the dark. It was tough going in the shoes I had on, too. I stuffed the dress in the trash and cried myself to sleep." She pursed her lips. "Now I wish I had punched her in the nose instead."

Simon wrapped her more tightly in his arms and nuzzled her cheek. "So that was why you got so prickly when I called you Secondhand Rose."

Roseanna hadn't meant to reveal so much tonight, but was glad she had. She suddenly realized she trusted Simon enough to allow their relationship to grow to a deeper and more meaningful level. It was as though he possessed some magical key that unlocked her heart, opening her to all the love waiting there inside.

"I expect to hear something from you now," she demanded, nudging him in the side and giving him an expectant smile.

"What do you want to know?"

She shrugged. "What's your favorite fish?"

"Tuna—raw. As in sushi."

"So, you're a gourmet." She nodding, thinking. "What was your favorite sport when you were ten?"

"Sailing and skiing. Things I could do by myself."

"An individualist, too. What were you like at eighteen?"

"I was an idiot mostly, when I wasn't acting like a moron." He rolled his eyes in self-deprecation. "Dad gave me an expensive red sports car for graduation."

"That was a foolish thing to do." She laughed, then sobered. "Seriously, what was it like for you growing up?"

A line furrowed between his brows. "Hmm. What was it like? Well, each of my three sisters and I had our own rooms, designed by a decorator. We had everything we needed and then some. The only problem was that our parents weren't here much. We were fortunate if they came home in time to tuck us in. They were consumed with their careers, and left us pretty much to be raised by a series of housekeepers and nannies."

"That sounds lonely," Roseanna said, empathy for him squeezing her heart.

"Sometimes we wondered why our parents bothered to have us."

"My family life was just the opposite," Roseanna remarked. "We had barely money enough to get by, but Mom was there for us always. In fact now I think the reason she didn't marry again after Dad died was because she never took the time to date. She was always at home helping us with schoolwork, or going to our activities, or just spending time with us. She never had a life of her own, separate from us."

Simon shook his head, a wry lift to his mouth. "We had the classic childhoods, only exactly opposite."

"But your father seems so different from how you just described him. You two spend time together and appear to have a great relationship," Roseanna observed, puzzled.

"After my mother's car accident Dad worked harder than ever. If he'd slowed down he would have had time to think, to face his feelings." Simon sighed. "All the stress and overwork . . . it was probably a factor in the heart attack. His father had died at fifty-five from heart failure. So when Dad's doctor told him it was usually the second heart attack that was fatal, he got scared."

"Scared enough to stop."

"And to reflect, at last," Simon concurred. "I think he was truly regretful not to have spent more time with us when we were kids. One day I found him crying, and he admitted how bad he felt. He wanted desperately to be a part of our lives."

She hugged Simon close. "And you let him be."

"Yes, of course," he replied matter-of-factly, as

though holding a grudge was inconceivable to him. "He also hadn't been excited about his work as an attorney for a long time, and one day he decided to pack it in. He made a vow to do only what he loved, from that moment on. Now he spends a lot of time with my sister's two boys, helping me at the shop, and sailing his boat, the *Swallow.* He always talked about how much he loved the Chesapeake Bay, how he had practically grown up on the water as a kid. His childhood dream was to own a fantastic boat. He worked hard, got his prize, and then like so many people, got caught up in his success and never had the time to enjoy it." Simon shook his head, his lips pressed tightly together. "I could count on my fingers the number of times we took the *Swallow* out when I was a boy. He didn't have the time to teach me to sail, but he could afford expensive sailing lessons. I learned more in sailing classes than I did from my own dad."

"That's so sad," Roseanna said, hugging Simon close.

"It was." He paused long enough to hug her back and brush a soft kiss against her forehead. "All that's changed now though. We go out as often as we can. Dad and I have become very close. I'm grateful for that."

"What a touching story. You are lucky."

"My dad learned his lesson about what was most important in life, and he didn't want me following in his footsteps in that regard. He was the one who encouraged me to sell my interest in the accounting firm to Janelle when we split. He knew that wasn't where my true interest lay. He was the one who reminded me that life was short, that it was about following your heart. And for once, I listened to him. Oakes Antiques is a dream come true."

Roseanna heard the doors opening behind them. She and Simon both turned to see Andrew beckoning them inside, his expression showing no reaction to having caught her and Simon huddled together.

"I'm sorry to call you in on such a splendid night, but dessert is ready."

Simon and Roseanna had just returned to their seats when Andrew arrived carrying a tray of crystal goblets filled with something icy and red.

"Raspberry sorbet," he announced, setting the dessert on the table. Andrew beamed at Roseanna. "I'm so glad Simon found someone who likes my cooking, which has been, by the way, all low fat. Even the cookies were made with fruit sauces instead of oil." He tapped his chest. "Doc said to cut down on the fats, to keep the old ticker in good shape."

"Everything you cook is delicious," Roseanna enthused.

"I'm glad you think so. We'll try lunch aboard my boat next time." He placed a dish in front of her. "Do you sail?"

"I've only gone once. I liked it a lot."

"Wonderful, wonderful. She loves my cooking, boats, and with a store like Treasures, she certainly must love old things." He nodded sagely to his son. "This girl is wonderful, my boy."

Roseanna flicked a horrified glance toward Simon, only to discover him grinning, his eyes twinkling. She smiled, and he coughed to cover his chuckles. His mirth was infectious. When her eyes met his, giggles bubbled up and began to spill out.

Andrew looked from one to the other, a mystified expression on his face. "What? What is it?"

Simon and Roseanna were laughing too hard to answer.

Chapter Seven

Roseanna came wide awake from a deep sleep. Not sure what woke her, wondering if she were hearing noises downstairs again, she propped herself up and rubbed her tired eyes. The clock on the nightstand said it was barely past six in the morning, too early to get up, so she burrowed back under the comforter. A sharp pinging sound had her shooting upward again.

Throwing on her bathrobe, she tiptoed across the chilly hardwood floor. Just as she approached the window a pebble hit the glass and she gasped in surprise.

She pushed up the window and peered into the early dawn light. The cool morning air brushed against her cheeks, chasing away any remaining sleepiness. In the shadowy side yard below her she made out the form of a tall man.

"Roseanna, it's me."

She recognized the deep voice at once, and her heart began to pound. "Simon! What are you doing down there?"

"I tried knocking. You must have been sound asleep."

"I was!"

"I need to talk to you."

"Do you realize what time it is?" She wondered if there was some emergency.

"Come down."

"All right." She hurried down the stairs to the outside entrance and unlocked the door. The sight of Simon took her breath away.

She had not heard from him since she'd had dinner at his father's house, several nights ago. She thought her feelings for Simon were under control, but one look into his eyes was enough to convince her otherwise. *Liar, liar,* her thumping heart taunted her.

"What are you doing here?" she got out, the squeaky tone of her voice embarrassing. He leaned a hand against the doorjamb and looked down into her eyes, causing her pulse to skyrocket. "It's six in the morning," she informed him.

"I would have called last night, but I only have your store number," he said.

"Is something wrong?"

"No, no. Sorry for scaring you, but we need to get an early start."

Not comprehending, Roseanna shook her head. "Either I'm still half asleep or you're not making any sense."

"I want to take you to an estate sale."

"An estate sale?" she repeated, shivering. It was excitement at seeing Simon, as much as the early morning chill, that was making her shake. She drew her robe up closer to her chin.

"You're cold. Let's go up, and I'll explain."

His surprise appearance had thrown her off balance, making it difficult to think clearly. "Oh, ah, sure," she murmured, finally getting her limbs to move. Peeling her hand off the knob, she motioned for him to follow her upstairs. By the time they reached her living room, the cobwebs in her mind had begun to clear.

"Make yourself at home," she said. "I'll go change."

After dressing in tan trousers and short-sleeved blouse, she came down the hallway to find Simon looking around. She had removed all of her aunt's old things, then cleaned and painted every surface before moving in. Numerous lush houseplants and colorful posters of elegant women in sleek, high-fashion gowns helped the large space feel cozy. She didn't have a lot of furnishings, but was proud of the fact that what she did have had come new from the store.

He picked up one of the fashion magazines that were forever scattered across the glass-topped coffee table. The cover sported a voluptuous model clad in a skimpy lime-green dress. The titles of the articles screamed out. *White-Hot Summer Wardrobe. Skinny Clothes, Fat Clothes. Fashion Secrets of the Stars.*

Roseanna felt a hot flash of embarrassment. She wished she hadn't already taken her other reading material back to the library. How limited he must think her interests were. "I like to keep up with current styles," she explained, adding a bit limply, "for when I get my boutique."

"You should see my collection of antiques magazines and books." He dropped the journal back onto the pile and glanced about him. "I like your place."

"No doubt you'd mix in a few antiques."

He grinned. "Probably more than a few. I like what you've done, though. It's simple and tasteful."

"Thanks," she said, feeling inordinately pleased by his compliment. "I'll make us some coffee."

"Sounds great."

Simon seated himself at her kitchen counter, and when she passed by him her nerve endings reacted wildly to the slight provocation. She retrieved the coffee bag from the refrigerator, feeling as though he were watching her every move. As she measured, the bag slipped, spilling grounds all over the countertop.

"Darn it!" She grabbed a sponge and pushed the mess into the sink. On her second attempt, she barely managed to get the coffee into the pot. This was ridiculous.

"Need some help?" he drawled.

Help was what she needed all right . . . help in resisting him. By biting down on her lip and focusing her attention, she managed to fill the coffeemaker with water. "I think I've got it licked now. Tell me about the estate sale."

"I was out on a buying trip yesterday. When I stopped at the town of St. Michael's, over on the Eastern Shore, I saw signs advertising a sale at a farm. I went out, and the owner was kind enough to give me a preview—even though he wouldn't let me purchase anything then. He said he wanted to wait and give everyone a fair chance. I saw a lot of antiques at bargain prices. Naturally, I thought of you."

"You want to share the goods?" She flashed him a curious look over her shoulder. "That's very generous of you."

"The way I see it, the better you do, the better I'll do. There are antiques and customers enough for both of us."

She got a carton of cream from the refrigerator. "Do you really feel that way?"

"Yes, I do." He paused before adding, "Even if I didn't, I'd want to help you anyway."

Feeling her face turning pink with delight, she turned to get two ceramic mugs out of the cupboard. The coffee began to drip into its glass carafe, filling the air with its fragrance.

"How about it," he asked. "Interested?"

"Yes, yes I am. Lately I've been wondering how to go about buying more antiques to mix with the secondhand stuff. I've seen how people coming to my store like it, and how they keep returning in hopes of finding a treasure among the other stuff."

"I think you're on to something."

"Is this farm hard to find?" Roseanna asked, placing the cups on the counter between them. "I don't want to go on a wild goose chase."

His amber eyes melted into hers. "I meant for us to go together."

"Oh. Okay."

Simon's large, warm hand surrounded hers, causing her heart to trip over itself. "Good."

"I think, um, the coffee's ready," she murmured, slipping her fingers from beneath his. "I'll get cups that we can take with us."

"Can you get someone to watch the store?"

"Tim will. He always wants to come in." She picked up the phone.

Simon's brows lowered, and his expression became shadowed. "Why don't you ask your friend Karyn?"

"She likes to spend her weekends shopping for those old clothes she likes." Roseanna met his gaze directly. "What's wrong with Tim?"

Simon's expression hardened ever so slightly. "I don't know. It's nothing I can put my finger on. There's just something about him that bothers me."

She pursed her lips thoughtfully. "I know he's not the ideal helper. But I'm not sure what to do about him. He dresses pretty grubby and lacks sophistication. He's more of an artist type than a shopkeeper, I guess. If I intend to promote a new image, of funky cool instead of secondhand cheap, I want Tim to play his part."

"I could ask my dad," Simon suggested. "I don't think he would mind."

"No," Roseanna said, shaking her head. Guilty feelings pricked her. "I'm being unfair to Tim. He always needs extra money. He was a big help to my aunt, and to me also. He might be rough around the edges, but he's a good person."

Before Simon had a chance to comment she dialed Tim's number and had arranged for him to come in. He said he'd be happy to, his voice cheerful and upbeat. He had been such a great guy in these past months, she recalled.

"We'll need to take my car," Simon said. "The van is in the shop."

Roseanna recalled the ride in his luxury sedan the night of his father's dinner. "How can we haul back all the loot in a car? If you're game, we'll go in my van."

"I didn't know you had one," he said, following her out of the building and into the parking area.

"I just bought it. The store is doing so well I decided to trade in my compact and get something more useful." She took him to a battered, dull green van parked in the back of her lot. "I call it Frog. I couldn't afford to buy new. Frog is a bit beat up, but he runs well."

"As long as it doesn't jump."

Roseanna wondered if Simon would change his mind when he saw the vehicle's ripped seats and inhaled the musty scent, but he climbed in without hesitation, as though he rode in fifteen-year-old vehicles every day of his life.

The first stop was at the cash machine at her bank downtown, where Roseanna skimmed as much from her account as she dared. She drove past the gift shops and boutiques concentrated around Main Street and the city dock area. Simon, with his passion for anything old, must love it in Annapolis, she mused, wishing she could see the eighteenth-century buildings through his eyes. When he began pointing out the colonial architecture as though she were a tourist, she nodded and smiled happily. Her ambivalent feelings toward him didn't keep her from feeling thrilled to be with him this morning.

After stopping for a fast-food breakfast, she drove them out of town. The sun was rising in a cerulean sky, and it promised to be a gorgeous May morning. Simon, looking relaxed in the passenger seat, tuned the radio to a country station.

"I grew up with that kind of music," she said, too keyed up to remain quiet for long. She regretted having consumed such a large cup of coffee. Being with Simon made her feel as jittery as if she had injected the caffeine directly into her veins.

"Not me," Simon said. "My mother used to drag us to classical music concerts. I suppose it was good for me, but I could never stop fidgeting. I finally threw such a fit she gave up and let me stay home. I started listening to country then, along with rock and blues. I like everything now—even classical."

Roseanna found herself relaxing, enjoying the drive and Simon's companionship as they discussed music, their stores, and then the oystermen who fished the local waters in their traditional skipjacks.

In no time they were crossing the bridge spanning Chesapeake Bay to the scenic, rural Eastern Shore. When they pulled into the farm she discovered they were the first to arrive.

"Are we too early?" she asked, worried about offending the farm owners.

"In this business, the early bird really does get the worm."

She started toward the house, but Simon snagged her hand and led her in the direction of a big, old barn.

"Come with me," he said.

Mesmerized by the feel of his fingers interlaced with hers, Roseanna followed him through the open barn doors and into the dim interior. Besides a few fat white hens that raced away clucking in indignation at the intrusion, they were alone. The wonderful smell of hay tickled her nostrils. Sunlight sliced through the gaps in the siding, illuminating particles of dust stirred up by the chickens. It was just an old barn, but with Simon pressed close to her side it seemed like they had entered a magical place.

The sound of soft mewling caught her attention, and next to empty horse stalls she spied a large cage with something moving inside. A sign saying FREE in red poster paint leaned against it.

"Oh look, Simon, kittens." She went over and crouched beside it, cooing at the darling creatures. They blinked up at her with large curious eyes, making her yearn to take all three in her arms.

"Aren't they adorable?" she said, as he knelt beside her.

He put a finger inside the wires and a tabby with white feet pounced playfully. "Frisky little guy," he remarked, chuckling.

"I've been thinking of getting a cat," she told him. "My landlord said it would be okay." Roseanna looked over, and when her gaze tangled with Simon's her heart lurched. Her eyes wandered down to his lips and lingered there, the memory of their kisses seeming as fresh as if they had happened only moments ago.

She saw a muscle twitch in Simon's jaw before he turned his gaze back to the kitten. "Ouch, this tiger can bite already." He withdrew his finger and shook it, feigning great pain. Rising, he held out his hand for her and pulled her to his side. "Look over here."

He took her to the rear of the barn. "Old farm equipment!" she exclaimed.

On a row of tables made from plywood and saw-horses was a fantastic assortment of goods. There were old pitchforks, leather harnesses stiff with age, and wooden buckets. She disentangled her fingers from Simon's and picked up a dusty oil lantern. "I could sell this in a minute." She checked the price sticker. "Not a giveaway, but very reasonable."

The barn turned out to be a treasure trove. Before any one else even discovered the place, Roseanna and Simon had made numerous trips to the van, each making a pile of the items they intended to buy.

"Here comes the owner," Simon said as he helped carry out a hand-built workbench he had persuaded her to take. A middle-aged man wearing slacks and button-down shirt made his way out to them. His harried expression changed to a smile as he approached.

"All this yours?" He addressed the question jointly to Roseanna and Simon as they set down the bench. She realized they must appear to be husband and wife.

Roseanna wiped her brow. The sun shone brightly above them and the morning grew warmer by the minute. A newfound sense of excitement rose as she prepared to dicker with him. "It is if we can agreed on a price. Do you own this farm?"

"It belonged to my grandfather, who just passed away. The folks are gone, too." He stuffed his hands in his trouser pockets, his expression showing mild distress. "My wife doesn't want any of this old stuff. We live in the city. Our place is very modern."

Roseanna understood his wife's position, since she had always felt the same way, wanting only new things. Yet, the man was selling off his heritage, and that saddened her.

She ran a hand over the rough surface of the workbench, feeling all the cracks and scars. The man's grandfather had probably used it everyday to build and repair things for the farm. What history this beat-up old bench contained. For the first time she thought of the used things in her store the way her customers must, as treasures instead of trash.

"I have cash." She handed the man her business card. "Let's make a deal."

As they negotiated a price it became clear money was of little importance to the seller. Roseanna could see he wanted to get his task finished and return to his life in the city. They quickly reached an agreement.

"I'd like one of the kittens in the barn, too," she said impulsively. "The tiger-striped one with the white feet."

"I'm afraid they've all been spoken for. A family with three little girls is taking them all."

Simon must have noticed her disappointed look because he reached over and gave her hand a consoling squeeze. When the farm owner departed, his gaze swept over all her purchases. "You have a real talent for this business," he said with admiration. "I'm impressed."

"Buy low, sell high is what Aunt Tildy always said," she chirped, grinning at him.

By noon she had only a hundred dollars left and felt exhilarated by what she had acquired. Humming gaily, she placed her final purchases—an old rocker, a washtub, and a wonderful crazy quilt—in the van. Clustered all around were larger pieces of furniture, mostly Simon's, that they did not have room for. Considering the amount of goods, she estimated they would have to make at least two more trips back here to collect it all.

"Are you finished?" he asked, as they pulled the van's doors closed.

"I had better be. I think I only have about ten dollars left," she said, laughing. "I'm going to take one more look in the house."

Simon had disappeared when she returned. After scouting around she found him behind the barn, leaning on a fence with one foot up on a weathered rail. Intent upon the verdant pasture that stretched out beyond them, he didn't hear her coming.

"Hungry?" she asked as she joined him.

He turned, his smile warming her more thoroughly than the midday sun. In one hand she offered for his inspection a cherry pie with a golden lattice top and bright-red filling. In the other she balanced a paper plate piled high with two fat sandwiches wrapped in plastic. Simon relieved her of the sturdy blanket and two icy cans of soda she had wedged under her arm.

"An enterprising neighbor was having a bake sale in the backyard," Roseanna explained. "I had the blanket already in the van. The owner told me where to go for a picnic. Are you in a hurry to get back to town?"

"I'd planned on spending the day with you."

Had he been so certain of her? She nodded toward the treetops just visible above a rise. "Just on the other side of that hill is a pond."

With Simon leading the way, they set off through the field, walking single file down a narrow path through the knee-high grass. A swollen-bellied chestnut mare some distance away lifted her head to watch their progress, but soon lost interest and went back to grazing. A sense of sleepy tranquillity hung over everything.

"This is perfect," Roseanna said, choosing a spot beneath a willow at the edge of the serene pool. They spread the blanket and laid out their lunch.

While devouring the sandwiches, they discussed the business of selling antiques and collectibles. Simon made it sound so fascinating that Roseanna found herself truly interested and plied him with question after question.

Lunch lingered on as they talked and ate. "I'm so glad I came today," Roseanna told him after finishing her last bite. "I've had a wonderful time."

Not appearing to be in any hurry to depart, Simon reclined close to her and began toying with her hair. "I'm glad, too," he murmured, his tone enflaming her senses.

She reached for the pie and placed it between them. Simon dug out a bright-red mound with a plastic fork and held it temptingly before her mouth. Roseanna took the offering, savoring the sweet-and-tart flavor.

When they'd had their fill, they went to wash their

hands in the pond. Feeling full of high spirits, Roseanna crouched close to the surface.

"Golly, look at that," she exclaimed, pointing down.

Simon moved closer. He heard her break into giggles, but before he could react she swiped at the water
and flicked cold droplets at his nose.

Not giving him a chance to retaliate, Roseanna
leaped up like a rabbit and dashed back to the blanket.
There, she flopped down, still laughing.

Simon reached the blanket and stood over her. How
beautiful she looked with her red hair blazing like fire
in the brilliant sunlight. Her eyes sparkled and danced
in a way that was slowly driving him mad. He had
heard the expression "smiling eyes" but had never
seen someone to whom it could be applied, until now.

He sat down beside her, leaning back on his elbows.
Knowing that if he continued to look at her he would
surely do something he would regret later, he kept his
gaze glued to the blue sky. Insects buzzed around
them, and the sun grew hotter as they talked and
laughed. He could not remember when he had last felt
so relaxed, yet so vibrantly alive.

Roseanna yawned broadly and stretched. "If I lie
here much longer I'm going to go to sleep."

"Is it my company?"

She wrinkled her nose at him. "Hardly. I keep hearing sounds coming from the store at night. Last night,
something woke me up at about three in the morning.
I actually got up the nerve to go down there and in-
vestigate, but nothing was amiss."

"Let me get this straight." His brow was furrowed

over his intense eyes. "You went down there in the middle of the night . . . alone?"

"Tim says it's just mice. He told me that my aunt had a bad problem with them."

Simon puffed out a breath, his exasperated expression making her feel stupid. "Or it could have been a punk kid breaking in, armed with a baseball bat."

"I've been hearing strange noises ever since I moved in," she quickly assured him. "Nothing has ever been disturbed. I'm sure Tim's right. It just gets to me sometimes."

He squeezed her hand in a comforting gesture. "I didn't mean to alarm you. Just don't you dare go traipsing about in the middle of the night. Call me. Any time."

She was close, reclining next to him. He blinked and stared at her face, her slightly parted lips an open invitation. She lay very still, as though she were caught like himself in a moment of swirling indecision. Her half-hooded eyes had turned a deep smoky gray, and he saw in them the same mix of longing and confusion he felt.

"What is it?" Roseanna murmured, feeling drunk from the intensity of his gaze.

Before she realized what was happening he was drawing her toward him, and she felt as helpless as a puppet, unable to resist his magic touch. Oh, how she yearned for him to kiss her.

Succumbing to the feelings roaring inside her, she let her eyelids drift closed. She could scarcely inhale, so achingly sweet was the anticipation.

At last their lips met in mutual surrender, the impact

of the sensation dissolving the strength from her body. She sank against him, and he began moving his mouth against hers. Without thinking, she wound her fingers around the back of his neck, encouraging him.

When the kiss ended she lay weakly against him, and he held her close, as though he feared she might evaporate if he loosened his grip. His cheek rubbed against hers, feeling slightly rough and angular.

Concentration knitted his brow, and his hooded eyes looked fierce. He seemed deep in thought, although how he managed any lucidity at the moment was quite beyond her. Her mind floated in the languorous stillness that hung over the pasture.

"Roseanna, Roseanna. What am I going to do with you?"

"Kiss me again?" she replied, smiling at him, feeling breathless and wonderful.

"Yes, definitely kiss you again."

Roseanna let him draw her into a sitting position, and she curled her legs beneath her. Tenderly, he brushed hair off her flushed cheek, his fingers warm and slightly rough against her sensitized skin. She gazed into his eyes, and in the dark pupils saw her feelings mirrored back.

He held her tight. "I told myself this wasn't going to happen." Then his mouth found hers again, and he didn't release her until several moments later. With her face buried in his neck, she took several deep breaths in an attempt to regain her equilibrium.

"Perhaps you should know we're being watched," he whispered.

"What?" Startled, Roseanna looked up to see the

chestnut mare, a few feet away. So that was their observer. When the mare stepped closer and lowered her blazed face in curiosity, Roseanna stroked her velvety muzzle, taking a moment to compose herself.

After satisfying her curiosity, the mare wandered off, and Roseanna flicked a shy glance at Simon. "Maybe we should get going."

"What's your hurry?" He responded, his voice like liquid velvet to her senses.

She smoothed her hair back in an attempt to tidy it. "We still have a couple of more trips to make back here."

Simon squinted up at the sun, wishing he could make it halt its progress across the sky. He could not, however, and time was passing. Besides showing her the sale, there was a reason he had wanted to see Roseanna today.

He caught her hand. "I want you to tell me what it is about me that's been bothering you."

Chapter Eight

Simon had caught her by surprise. He watched her lips partially open and then close. Reaching for her hand, he stroked the smooth skin. He liked her hands, delicate and yet strong, like Roseanna herself.

As his question hung in the air between them, he waited, determined to get an answer before leaving. The uncertainty of their relationship was driving him crazy. He had to know where he stood with her.

"Are you going to tell me?" he persisted.

She flicked a glance at him out of the corner of her eye. "What do you mean?" she asked, her voice falsely light.

"That night we went out for coffee, something happened," he pointed out. She tensed, and he continued to grip her hand for fear if he let loose she might bolt like a skittish doe. "You began to act differently. Was it something I did? Something I said?"

She pasted on an unbelievable smile. "You were a perfect gentleman. Really."

"I'm not imagining this," he pressed.

"I can be moody." She was trying hard to sound lighthearted. "That's all. You know how women are."

He caressed her wrist. "Roseanna," he murmured. "You are not moody. I don't believe that."

He watched as the smile slid from her mouth. Her blue eyes became murky and distant, her long dense lashes lowering to conceal the troubled emotions he saw churning there.

Simon was content to wait her out. She fidgeted, but made no attempt to get up. Catching her gaze, he looked deeply into the pain he saw there.

"Tell me what's going on."

She lifted her slender shoulders in a half shrug and grimaced. "I'm sorry I've behaved oddly. You do deserve to know." She drew in a deep breath. "The truth is . . . it's just that . . . I like to think I'm the kind of person who learns her lesson, who doesn't keep repeating mistakes."

He frowned at her, not understanding. "Am I a mistake?"

"Yes," she blurted out, almost angrily. "Yes, you are." She moaned in frustration and with her free hand rubbed her temples. "At least I think you might be. And that terrifies me."

She looked away with an abrupt motion. Simon studied her face, searching for the sweet, open expression that made her so appealing. But her features had become a mask, the pretty curve of her mouth a thin line. She stared out to where the blue sky met the green pasture as though she wished she were there on the horizon, far away from him.

He wove their fingers together. "Go on," he urged in gentle tones.

"You see, I promised myself I wouldn't become involved with a divorced man."

He considered that for a moment. "Some guy— some divorced guy—gave you a hard time, and so you decided that men who had been previously married were trouble."

She cleared her throat. "Bingo." Her gaze flicked to his, lingered long enough to reveal her distress, then shot away again.

"And if a man with blond hair was the culprit you'd reject all other blonds, right?"

She carefully extracted her fingers from his and crossed her arms, as though she wanted to wall herself off from him. "You know that's not the same. You're not being fair."

"I'm trying to understand you. Come on," he coaxed. "Will you tell me what happened?"

Her lips compressed again. "I would really rather not."

He waited for more, but the silence stretched on and on. A chasm had opened up between them, threatening to become a dark, gaping, endless divide in their relationship. She stood on one side and he was on the other. The helplessness he felt frightened him.

"Is that it?" he pressed, his voice sharper than he had intended. "Is that all the explanation I deserve?"

"Please," she whimpered. "Can't we just forget it?"

The stubborn set of her mouth, the same mouth that had moments ago so eagerly responded to his kisses, was starting to drive him mad.

Thinking over her refusal, he began to have the distinct feeling that if he did not find a way to break down her barriers their relationship would come to a final, grinding halt right here in this beautiful pasture. Should he allow that to happen? Did he want to be done with this obstinate little redheaded female? Or should he put up a fight? If it were another woman, he wouldn't even consider prying into her private affairs. But this was Roseanna, and that made everything different. Until that very moment he hadn't realized just how deeply involved he had become.

What he must do was clear: break through her protective barriers and show her she could trust him. How to do so was another matter. He sat for a while with his gaze focused on nothing in particular as he gathered his thoughts. Finally, he had an idea. Turning toward her, he waited until she at last relented and looked at him.

"When I was in first grade I tried to share crayons with a freckle-faced girl in pigtails, but she only stuck her tongue out at me," he told her.

Roseanna's brow creased. "Huh?"

He plucked a piece of long grass. "When I was fourteen I kissed Priscilla Parker at the school dance. She slapped my face, right in front of everybody." Simon noticed that Roseanna's frozen expression was begin-

ning to thaw in curiosity. Warming to his subject, he
continued, "When I was sixteen, I managed to get gorgeous Leslie Buttons alone on her family's cabin
cruiser and everything was going great . . . until her
six-foot-four, ex-linebacker father arrived on the
scene."

Roseanna cracked a smile.

He winked. "Want to know what happened?"

She grinned. "Of course."

"I'll tell you if you tell me," he challenged. "I've
just related three of the most embarrassing romantic
situations in my life. Now it's your turn."

"It's not the same," she protested.

"True," he admitted, puffing out a breath. "All right.
I'll tell you why I got divorced." He felt the old familiar hardening inside his heart, the walling off of his
emotions that had once provided some relief from the
pain of Janelle's betrayal. He had told no one the
whole story, not even his family. He cleared his throat
and concentrated on the slender fingers twined with
his own. He could do this, he told himself. "Janelle
and I married fresh out of college. I thought we had
the world by the tail, but I really had no idea who I
was or what I wanted out of life. Janelle was fiercely
ambitious. She had expectations of me that I busted
my butt to fulfill. Then one day, after having a heart-
to-heart with my dad, it was as though I had woken
up from a bad dream. I realized I was becoming what
my parents had been, workaholics striving to get . . ."
He shrugged. "What? More? More money? More
status? More what? I was sick of it all. I wanted out.
I wanted to work with the antiques that I loved and

the heck with everyone who thought I had gone around the bend. What a shock for Janelle. She simply could not comprehend it." He laughed, but it was not a humorous sound. The blade of grass he was twisting in his fingers had become frayed and broken. "I was still hoping to work things out when she told me she was leaving me for one of our clients."

"Oh, Simon, I'm so sorry."

He threw the grass away. "And that's the end of my oh-so-tragic tale."

A gentle breeze pushed a wisp of shining auburn hair across her face. He noticed how the sun was creating an appealing pink glow to her cheeks, making her look radiantly healthy. How could someone manage to be so uncomplicated and yet so complex at the same time?

He captured her hand and caressed it. "Now it's your turn."

She stared at his hand on hers before looking up to meet his gaze. He smiled softly in encouragement.

"You didn't tell me what happened when Leslie Button's father came on board."

He cracked a grin. "I escaped out the forward hatch and swam for it."

"Did you see her again?"

He cocked a brow. "Or did I decide all girls who had big fathers were off limits?"

She made a face and punched him in the side with her elbow.

He grinned at her. "The very next weekend I went to her house and asked to take her out. The old man was pretty amazed to see me show up in his living room. I guess he figured if I possessed the nerve to face him I must be a decent kid after all."

"That took a lot of courage."

"Yep." He sobered. "I guess I realized early on it's the only way I could face life and survive."

"All right," she said with a sigh. "I'll tell you about Gary."

Simon listened in respectful silence as she unraveled her tale. "In the end," she finished, "I realized it was a rebound relationship. Gary used me to soothe his torn-up heart. His divorce left him mixed up and hurting and feeling rotten about himself. I made him feel better—at least for a while. He told me he loved me. But it was obviously not enough to trust me. When he accused me of cheating on him—" She clamped her quivering lips together. When Simon saw tears shimmering in her eyes it was all he could do to keep from gathering her into his arms. "Perhaps I should be grateful. Being dumped the day before your wedding is definitely preferable to the day after."

He shook his head and frowned. "I can only imagine how awful that must have been for you."

"Gary had gotten in deep before he realized he didn't really love me. I think accusing me of betrayal was just his cowardly way of getting off the hook."

"Now you don't trust 'secondhand men.' "

She nodded. "That's the reason I've acted strangely around you sometimes. I've felt so confused. I, uh, care for you very much . . . but I don't know if I want to have a relationship that is more than just friendship."

Now that he knew the problem, the bottomless

chasm he had imagined between them began to shrink. Their problems were not insurmountable. He knew that with enough time and tender loving care he could convince her to open her heart to him. "Being just friends is not what I had in mind for us," Simon murmured.

Immediately, Roseanna's cheeks turned vibrant pink. "That's what I suspected," she mumbled, looking anywhere but at him.

He leaned nearer and nuzzled her hair, taking devilish delight in her discomfort. "Because I kissed you?"

"Um . . ." Her tongue darted out nervously to moisten her lips. "Yes, I suppose."

"Or was it the *way* in which I kissed you?" he whispered in her ear.

"Simon, this is not helping," she protested, scooting away from him.

"What do you want to do?" he asked. "Do you want to keep seeing me?"

She hesitated long enough to cause him to worry.

"I do." The confession came out on a wobbly breath. "But it scares me."

"Me, too."

Capturing her waist, he pulled her into his embrace, his mouth taking hers. When their lips finally parted he held her for a long while, rocking her in a slow and gentle motion. Then he leaned back and scrubbed the hair from her face. "Ah, Roseanna. Trying to fend off her Secondhand Simon," he mocked her tenderly.

"Oh!" She erupted, pushing him away to rise unsteadily to her feet. "If you're trying to win me over, Mr. Oakes, *that* is not the way to do it!"

"Hello, up there." Simon had walked through the double doors, open to let in the warm summer afternoon.

"Hello, down there," Roseanna chirped in reply, looking down at him from her perch atop a stepladder nearby.

Even though she had seen him nearly every day during the three weeks since their outing to the farm sale, her heart still raced whenever he was near.

"Wow, these are incredible," he exclaimed as he walked beneath the eight-foot-tall wooden palm trees she was erecting beside the front doors. "Where did they come from?"

Roseanna finished threading wire through the eye bolt in the ceiling before climbing down. She had not really needed to secure the plywood trees from above, since they already had sturdy bases, but she had wanted to make sure the heavy decoration would not fall over and clobber a customer.

"I hired Tim to make them for me."

"Whose idea was it?" he asked, admiring them.

"Mine. But Tim and I did spend a lot of time deciding what they would look like and how to construct them," she replied, pleased that he liked them. "I haven't told you because I wanted it to be a surprise. I'm adding to my pirate theme. Underneath the trees I'm going to pour mounds of sand and put out a sea chest displaying costume jewelry."

He chuckled. "I like it."

"What brings you over today?" she asked conversationally, placing her wire and cutters into her new toolbox. She did not really need to ask. They had become accustomed to each other's casual, unexpected visits. By now she was disappointed when they didn't occur.

"Well . . . it's a little hard to explain. Why don't you come out to my car with me, and I'll show you."

"Hmm. This is interesting," she said, her curiosity piqued.

It had been a quiet day and there were no customers in the store at the moment, so Roseanna followed him out to the parking area. When they arrived at his car, he nodded for her to look through the window. She stepped up next to him and peered inside.

A black cat that was larger than some breeds of dogs sat on the driver's seat and glared at her with wicked yellow eyes. A leash dangled from his red nylon collar.

Roseanna blinked in surprise. "What's this?"

"A cat." Simon grinned.

She rolled her eyes. "I can see that."

"He's not mine." Simon sighed and braced his hands on his hips. His shoulders looked even broader than usual, his arms impressive in his short-sleeved summer shirt. "The manager at my apartment complex found him in a vacated unit. He couldn't find the owner and pets aren't allowed, so he intended to get rid of it at the animal shelter. As a not-too-friendly adult cat, I didn't think his chances would be very good for adoption."

"And you thought of me. You remembered how

much I wanted that kitten," Roseanna concluded, her
heart sinking.

Her feelings must have shown in her face because
his expression suddenly clouded. "If you don't want
him, please don't feel you have to take him. I just
thought I'd give it a shot."

She chewed on her lip. The truth was she did not
want him. She had yearned for a kitten fresh from its
mother, not a grown cat who was someone else's discard.

She had realized by now how greatly she was influ-
enced by her past and decided she did not like it. Still,
those old feelings lingered. Struggling with her emotions, she stared bleakly through the window glass at
Simon's passenger. Unaware that this human could
well be deciding his fate, the animal returned the pe-
rusal with intense suspicion.

"Don't you know anyone else who might want
him?" Hoping to be let off the hook, she tried, "What
about your dad? He could probably use some company."

"Allergic." Simon frowned, rubbing his jaw. "I wish
I could think of someone." After a moment of silence,
he dug into his pockets for his keys. "Roseanna, I'm
sorry for putting you in this spot. I can see this cat is
not what you had in mind for a pet. Don't worry about
it."

She scrutinized his expression, expecting to detect
unfavorable judgment there. And although she saw no
hint of disappointment in his face, she felt it intensely
inside herself. Simon, as usual, was unwittingly chal-

lenging her to break down her self-imposed limitations.

As her emotions battled inside her, pushing her in all directions, Roseanna scrunched up her face in indecision. She did not want the animal—yet could not in good conscience send him off to an uncertain future.

"Okay," she blurted out. "I'll take him. After all, I have a secondhand store," she said with a disgruntled sigh. "I suppose it's only fitting to have a secondhand cat."

Simon didn't say a word, but his lips slowly curved upward. She stared at them, mesmerized, his simple smile washing over her like a brilliant ray of sunshine.

"Well, let's get the beast out of your car," she said, reaching for the door handle.

His hand stayed hers. "Better let me."

Roseanna stood aside to let Simon ease the door open. Being careful not to let the animal escape, he reached in and seized it around its formidable girth. Ten razor-sharp claws shot out, and an ominous growl rumbled forth. Instinctively, she took another step back.

"Easy, big guy." Seemingly undaunted by the protesting feline's threats, he cradled it under his arm like a football and round the leash around his hand.

"What's his name?" Roseanna asked as they headed back to the store. She tentatively reached over to pet him, but his flattened ears and warning hiss had her snatching her fingers to safety.

Simon shrugged. "I don't know."

She cocked her head, thinking. "Captain Blackbeard it'll be, then."

Simon chuckled. "You have a great imagination. That's perfect."

At Roseanna's request, Simon turned Blackbeard loose in the store. For a moment the creature froze, no doubt getting his bearings, then he arched his head forward and sniffed the air. Cautiously, he took a step forward, looked around to check behind him, then took another step. As long as she kept the doors closed he should not be able to escape.

Simon left, only to return an hour later carrying two large shopping bags.

"What now?" Roseanna teased, her blood racing to see him again so soon. She wondered if he had any idea how his unexpected appearances affected her. "A rabid cocker spaniel someone left on your doorstep?"

"Supplies." He handed her the bulky packages.

Inside one she found a deluxe plastic litter box and a mound of expensive canned cat food. The other contained a wicker bed with a blue-and-green plaid cushion, grooming articles, and a catnip-stuffed toy mouse.

"Oh, Simon," she said, laughing in delight at his extravagance. She set the packages on her desk. "You didn't need to do this. But thanks anyway."

"How is it going with the Captain?"

"He hid under that workbench I got at the farm and won't come out again." She crouched down to see if he was still there and was rewarded by a mean hissing for her effort.

She gasped and jerked back, bumping into Simon. He gripped her forearm to help her up. "Whoa," he muttered. "What a monster. I hope he settles down."

His concerned expression melted her heart. "Don't

worry," she said. "He'll be all right . . . and I think I'll be, too. Besides, my customers will like him. He looks like he belongs here somehow."

Simon released her arm and ran his hand along the rough surface of the workbench. "This looks great. All the antiques look good."

"They do. Thanks again for taking me to the farm. I had a wonderful time." Since then, they had spent every weekend together, going to all the estate sales and garage sales and flea markets they could squeeze in. "I've become a yard-sale junkie because of you."

"I'm beginning to think we could make a pretty good team."

"A team," she murmured, the words resonating against her heart. "I like that. How about this weekend, partner? Tim doesn't mind working. He's always eager for some extra money."

Simon's expression tightened. "Tim is good for the occasional handyman odd job, but why don't you find someone else to run the shop when you're gone? I know a nice older woman who is in the market for part-time employment. Kate once owned a small antiques and collectibles shop, so she's highly qualified. Are you interested?"

"Tim's feelings would be hurt."

"Roseanna." He sighed. "Are you a businesswoman or not? Tim is not cut out to be a salesman. You know that."

She recalled returning to the store more than once only to find Tim with his boots up on the desk engrossed in an art magazine while customers wandered about unnoticed. His attitude toward the job was laid back to say the least. Nevertheless, he had been a life-saver when she was struggling to get Treasures ready to open, and she felt she owed him a debt of gratitude.

"Here's Kate's number," Simon said, writing it on the back of one of his business cards. "Think it over."

Roseanna decided it was time to clear the air. "You've never liked Tim."

"Not much," he concurred in a matter-of-fact tone, not looking up.

"Why?"

"I can't put my finger on it. I just have a gut feeling something's not quite right about him."

"He's never been a problem," she defended Tim.

"I hope it stays that way." Simon drew her into his arms and looked down into her eyes. "I won't be seeing you for a couple of weeks. I'm going to Europe on an antique-buying trip. Dad is watching the shop for me." He smoothed her hair off her cheek. "I know it's sudden, but could you come?"

"To Europe?" The thought of going with Simon caused her to giggle in heady excitement. "When are you leaving?"

"Next week."

Temptation gripped her fiercely. Yet, she knew she could not. She had no money for it and wouldn't allow Simon to pay. "I wish I could."

Thankfully he didn't press. Instead he gathered her closer to him for a lingering kiss.

She wondered if the upcoming trip was what had caused Simon's uncomfortable feelings about Tim to rise to the surface. Did the idea of another male prowling about during his absence bother him? Could it be that Simon did not yet completely trust her?

Simon smiled down at her. "I'll miss you."

Melting into the warmth of his amber eyes, it was easy to forget the troubling questions. "I'll miss you, too," she murmured, her heart already starting to ache. "Very, very much."

By the day Simon was to return, Roseanna's nerves were jumping in anticipation of seeing him again. After she helped load a painting of Elvis on black velvet into a young woman's Volkswagen Beetle, Roseanna trudged through the sultry August heat back to the store. Once inside, she locked up, glad 5:00 had finally rolled around. She felt restless, anxious.

Roseanna called to Captain Blackbeard, who had slowly come to tolerate her, and carried him upstairs. There she fed him dinner and fixed a glass of iced tea for herself before going to change. She stripped down to her underwear and flopped onto the bed.

She stared at the phone on the nightstand, willing it to ring. *Come on, Simon, call me,* she begged silently. *Tell me how much you've missed me, too.*

When it did ring just then her heart nearly catapulted from her chest. She scrambled across the floral comforter to snatch up the phone—the most wonderful of all inventions—and rolled over with the receiver to her ear.

"Hi," she heard Simon's deep voice rumble across the wire. "I'm back. I want to see you."

"When?" she asked, breathless with excitement.

"Right away. Right now."

"Come over," she urged.

"Fifteen minutes," he said, then hung up.

Roseanna hugged the receiver, smiling in a goofy way up at the ceiling. He had not said the exact words she had wanted to hear, but the meaning was the same. He had missed her . . . very much.

A heady surge of anticipation replaced the biting loneliness of the last two weeks. Propelled by a flood of energy, she raced to the bathroom to freshen up. After scrubbing her face clean, she applied makeup with shaky fingers. She brushed her hair so fast it caused the strands to crackle with electricity. With no time to fix it into any style, she let it flow unhampered over her shoulders. Satisfied with her appearance, she pulled on a simple cotton dress. Then, she suddenly had nothing else to do. She began to walk back and forth in the hot apartment. As a trickle of perspiration inched its way down her neck, she grabbed her hair and held it up off her neck as she paced.

Spying Captain Blackbeard, she scooped him up into her arms and stroked his silky fur until he glared at her in agitation. Just as he had grown to accept her, she had come to admire and care for him. It did not matter anymore that he was a grown cat who had belonged to someone else before her. He was really a most expressive creature, so much more interesting than that kitten would have been. She let him jump down and smiled as she watched him strut away, tail twitching in indignation.

When being cooped up in the stuffy apartment finally became intolerable, she skipped down the stairs and waited in the shady courtyard.

At last she saw a familiar sedan coming down the street. She saw Simon driving. And he saw her. Their gazes held as he whipped into the parking lot and killed the engine. He stepped out and stared at her with an intensity that held her paralyzed except for the shallow breaths lifting her chest and the wild thumping of her heart.

He closed the distance between them with long strides and swept her up in his arms. At once his mouth descended and he kissed her fiercely, right in the parking lot.

When he finally released her she could not keep from staring at him, reassuring herself he was not just an apparition she had conjured up from sheer longing.

"You're glowing," he said, teasing her in a delightful way.

"So are you," she returned boldly.

His expression grew serious. "I'm glad to be back. I'm glad to see you again. It's been the longest two weeks I can remember ever having."

Her throat felt thick. "I know exactly what you mean."

As his presence filled the void inside her heart, an emotion began to build. It started at some mysterious place deep inside her and radiated outward to fill her with incredible joy. It was a frightening and exhilarating and wonderful feeling. At that moment she realized she had done what she had sworn not to do: she had fallen in love with a secondhand man.

Chapter Nine

It was a hot and humid August Monday morning when Roseanna decided to start cleaning out the basement. She had been thinking about it for weeks now, and often when she had a slow period at the store she would go down to the basement to poke around and ponder what to do with the space.

Meanwhile, she had continued to improve the upstairs store by constantly coming up with ideas on how to make it more interesting and, with Simon's input, more profitable. Aunt Tildy's Community Thrift Store had transformed into a one-of-a-kind shop, charming and fun and funky, a delight to Roseanna's customers. People loved Treasures, returned frequently, and brought their friends. The business was humming along nicely. Now Roseanna felt ready for a new challenge. And boy, was cleaning up the basement ever going to be one.

She and Tim stood at the bottom of the stairs assessing the task before them. The unadorned cement walls and floors seemed to soak up what little light there was like gray sponges. Cobweb-strewn broken furniture and dirty boxes filled with who-knew-what lay about in no order whatsoever.

Preparing herself to begin, Roseanna sucked in a deep breath. "Yuck. It smells musty down here. Let's open all the windows and get some fresh air, even if it is hot air."

"You got it," Tim said, yanking open the nearest one.

Roseanna pulled on the next one and they continued on around the room. The windows were small and set at street level, so if someone happened to walk past all you would see would be up to their knees.

"How's that, Babe?" Tim asked, propping open the last one.

"Hey bub, I'm not your babe." Roseanna tried to keep her voice light even though his endearment bothered her. Lately Tim had begun to flirt with her. She had dealt with his unwelcome attentions so far by simply ignoring them. Unless he began increasing the pressure she saw no reason to confront him and create more uncomfortable feelings between them. She had already had a talk with Tim about how she expected him to dress and behave when he minded the store for her. Although he had conformed adequately to her wishes, she sensed an unspoken resentment. She still had Kate's number, just in case Simon's instincts about Tim turned out to be right.

What was worse, she worried whether Simon had noticed Tim's gathering interest in her. Since their uncomfortable discussion about Tim before the trip to Europe, Simon had not mentioned the young man again. And neither had Roseanna.

"Why so sensitive? You still hot on that guy across the street?" Tim asked in a teasing tone.

"We're dating," Roseanna replied casually, not wanting to discuss her love life with him.

She wished Simon had been able to help instead of Tim, as he had done so often and so willingly throughout the summer, but he'd had an important appointment to view an estate some miles away and had to be gone most of the day. Besides, the idea of surprising him with a clean and empty basement was immensely appealing.

Tim removed his glasses and began to polish them on his sleeveless T-shirt. "Well then, maybe—"

"Come on," she cut him off, walking away. "We've got a big job ahead of us."

He sighed. "All right, Miss Slave Driver. What's first?"

Heading briskly through the basement with Tim trailing behind, she pointed to dilapidated cardboard cartons overflowing with yellowed newspapers. "That box goes, and that one over there, too."

"Where do you want me to take them?"

"Pile all the trash behind the building. We can load it into my van and haul it away later." She looked around at the colossal mess and hardened her resolve to get the place in order. "Right now I just want it out of here."

Tim hunkered down next to a two-foot-high pile of magazines. "What about these?"

Roseanna crouched beside him and picked up the top one, wrinkling her nose at the musty smell. Too old to be of interest and too new to be collectible, she determined, going on to the ones underneath. Then she hit several magazines with beautiful photographs on their front covers. These magazines, she knew, were very popular. Her fingers hesitated. Deciding they might have value, she placed them aside. Silently, she thanked Simon for her now-discerning eye. Last spring those magazines would have gone into the trash without a second thought.

After separating all the good ones, she tossed the worthless periodicals back into the box. A cloud of dust wafted upward, causing her to sneeze. As Tim caught her arm to steady her the emerald necklace she was wearing caught his gaze.

"I've seen you wearing that. What did you do, rob a bank or something?"

"It belonged to Aunt Tildy," Roseanna said, going on to tell where Simon had found it. She looked up to catch Tim staring at her with an odd intensity before he shifted his eyes away, and she wondered what he was thinking.

He shrugged in a nonchalant way. "Who knows why it was in that cabinet."

"I've always been curious about my eccentric aunt," Roseanna went on as she pulled over another box of magazines to sort through. "She never made a fortune with this old place, but she did okay, and she was very thrifty. I know she had money—but her bank account hardly had a penny in it when she died. We were all mystified. What could she have done with it?"

"Maybe she gave it to charity. I worked for your aunt, and I know what she was like. She was weird sometimes, but she was also one smart ol' cookie. I don't think she was the type to hoard her loot inside her mattress." He cocked a brow at Roseanna. "You checked the mattress, right?"

Guilty, Roseanna flushed in embarrassment. "When I was cleaning out the apartment I did find a tea tin with two hundred dollars in a cupboard. Also a cigar box filled with Indian-head pennies, buffalo nickels, and other valuable coins in the bedroom closet. And there was a gold brooch and wedding ring hidden in a sock drawer."

"So, you found a few things. Not exactly a fortune in treasure, though." He grinned and gave her a playful cuff on the arm. "She probably had a lot of expenses you didn't know about, or like I said, gave it away. With all the cleaning and organizing you've done, if your great-aunt had stashed her loot somewhere in the building you would have found it long ago."

"You're probably right," Roseanna agreed. "She was a strange lady, though."

"So are you."

"Me?"

Tim reached over and tapped the emerald necklace. "Don't you think it's just a little odd to wear jewelry that's worth as much as my clunker car while you're cleaning out the basement?"

"Pretty dopey, I agree." Smiling, she rose to her feet. "After these magazines and newspapers, let's take out those bundles of old rags. But leave the boxes of clothes. I want Karyn to look through them. She won't care if she finds Aunt Tildy's money. To her a poodle skirt or nineteen-fifties ball gown would be a treasure."

When Tim had departed up the stairs, his biceps bulging with his first load of trash, Roseanna took a moment to finger the necklace. She'd worn it every day since Simon's return. It reminded her of him—as if she needed reminding—and at the hard, cool feel of it her heart swelled with joy.

They had not spoken the words yet, but she was almost certain she could see his love for her shining in his eyes. The same wondrous love she felt for him. Now that she admitted it, it seemed as though the feelings had erupted overnight. Yet she knew it had actually been a slow opening of her heart to him. It seemed incredible to have fallen in love. It was so unexpected—even unwanted. Yet it had happened.

"Hey, Roseanna." Tim broke into her thoughts when he came bounding back down the stairs. "Would you mind paying me today when we're through? I'm broke as a dog." He seemed to hesitate, and then continued with a boyish grin, "Say, a friend is having a little get-together at his studio tonight. He's a cool dude. There'll be a lot of music and brew. Want to come?"

"Thanks, but I don't think so," Roseanna refused, keeping her voice light and easy. "I've got tons to do still. And Karyn is coming over tonight."

"She's welcome."

"Sorry."

He shrugged, his neutral expression not quite con-
cealing his disappointment. "No big deal. Tell me if
you're free some time."

"You bet." Pulling a heavy old book out of a carton,
she saw it was a water-damaged dictionary a few years
old and heaved it into the discard pile.

She threw herself back into sorting boxes, but her
mind wasn't on the task. She wanted to tell Tim
straight out that she was unavailable, but since she and
Simon had not yet discussed their relationship, she
could not in good conscience do so. Should she reveal
her heart to Simon? She yearned to do so. She was
bursting to confess. But even while she longed to admit all, another part of her warned to be cautious. No
matter what she might hope and no matter the passion
in his kisses, Simon had yet to declare any deep feelings for her.

When the box she had been working on had been
emptied she kicked it aside. Taking a breather, she
leaned against a wooden dining-room table whose
once gorgeous veneer was now buckled and peeling.
She ran her hands over the rough, warped top. Simon
had taught her a great deal about restoring furniture,
but this poor piece was just too badly damaged to sal-
vage. It could never be put right again.

Had Simon's heart also been broken beyond repair
when the woman he had loved betrayed him? Painful
doubts began to creep into her thoughts like stinging
wasps. Just because she wanted him to love her did
not mean that he did, the old fearful part of herself
warned.

Simon was a secondhand man, she reminded herself. Had he gotten over his divorce? Was she just a rebound relationship to him? Would he walk away with his ego inflated, while she suffered a shattered heart?

She shook her head, trying to get rid of the maddening questions. Her first experience with love had hurt. This one, so much more powerful, would devastate her if she were not careful. She must keep her feelings to herself, she decided, at least for the time being.

Roseanna and Tim worked in the basement until nearly 6:00. They had emptied the space of all the trash and had created an enormous pile of rubbish out back. The items Roseanna had decided to save—the mannequins, store fixtures, some magazines, clothes, and various pieces of furniture—had been placed to one side.

Sipping on an icy cola, she surveyed the large bare area, savoring her accomplishment. The warm breeze and the bright early evening sunlight entered through the windows they had opened earlier, creating an even more pleasant atmosphere. She couldn't wait to show Simon.

When they headed upstairs, leaving the cooler underground room, the air grew steadily hotter and muggier. The work had been physically draining, but Roseanna felt emotionally energized. Companionably, they walked together through the store. When Captain Blackbeard saw Tim he dove beneath a cabinet, his usual reaction to the young man. It seemed the Captain was as wary of Tim as Simon was.

Roseanna went over to coax out her pet. It was time to go upstairs for a well-deserved shower, and she wanted to take him with her.

She crouched down and tapped her fingers on the floor, trying to lure him. "Come on, Sweetie. Come here, Blacky."

When he backed further away, his yellow eyes glaring beyond her suspiciously at Tim, she leaned in after him. Suddenly the wood floorboard beneath her creaked and shifted. She leaned on the board again and it creaked a second time.

Tim came over. "What are you doing down there?"

"There's a loose board here," she answered.

"I'm not surprised. Everything is loose in this old place."

She saw that the plank was a short one, no more than a foot in length. It had probably been a patch. Curiously, she pried at the edge of the wood with her fingertips to see just how unsecured it was. The board lifted up readily, and what she saw tucked between the joists made her gasp in shock.

There, wrapped in clear plastic and secured with several rubber bands, huddled a bundle of dollar bills.

"Tim, look," she gasped, not quite believing what she saw.

Tim stared. "Is that what I think it is?"

"I never really thought . . ." She gingerly pulled out the package and dusted it off.

"Aren't you going to open it?" Tim demanded, as excited as she was. "How much do you think is there?"

"I have no idea." Adrenaline coursed through her

veins as she tore off the plastic covering to reveal a thick pad of green currency and a piece of covering paper. On the paper was written in her aunt's distinctive Spencerian script: *five thousand dollars.* She spread the bills in her hands like a deck of cards. Twenties. A lot of them. Still on her knees, she counted, her hands shaking. It was exactly five thousand dollars.

Clutching the bills in both hands she looked up at Tim and burst into giggles. Her head spun. "This is amazing."

Suddenly Tim had wrapped his arms around her in a sort of celebratory hug. Bursting into laughter, she hugged him back.

"Roseanna."

Through her mirth she heard Simon's voice, but it took her a moment to shift gears. Her arms fastened around Tim, she saw the tall dark-haired man standing nearby. His expression was unreadable, but his cool gaze sobered her at once. Awkwardly, she dropped her arms, and after a few seconds, Tim followed suit.

"Simon, I'm so glad to see you." She sounded breathless and silly. "I didn't expect you back so soon."

He braced his hands on his hips and cocked a brow. "I can see that."

"Look. We've just found a treasure. Real treasure!" She thrust the money into the air toward him. Tim rose to his feet then reached down to help her up, and she accepted his outstretched hand.

"Oh, your pay." She thrust some of the bills toward him.

Ignoring Simon, Tim caught her eye and gave her an intimate smile. "Thanks, Babe. I guess I'll head out. Phone you later."

Roseanna waited until she and Simon were alone before speaking. "Simon, there's nothing going on between—"

"You don't have to explain."

When she saw his face soften relief flooded through her, and her thoughts flew back to the money. Waving the bills in the air above her, she did a goofy little victory dance. "I can't believe it! I can't believe it! There was a loose board—Aunt Tildy must have hidden it there—oh, Simon . . . five thousand dollars!"

"Now that the competition is gone, I think it's my turn to hug you." He did and followed that with a thorough kiss. By the time he was finished with her, she was feeling giddier than ever. He leaned back and picked a cobweb out of her hair.

Roseanna realized what she must look like. With the back of a grubby hand she brushed the loose, limp tendrils of hair that had worked loose from her ponytail off her forehead. She examined herself and grimaced. Her arms and legs were grimy. Stains covered the middle of the old yellow top she wore, and she could only imagine what the seat of her cutoffs looked like.

"I'm a mess."

"I've never seen you more beautiful," Simon countered. He winked, adding, "Of course, I've always had a thing for rich women. Want to spend some time with me tonight? Since you're Miss Moneybags, you can treat me to dinner."

"Oh, Simon, I can't," she said with regret. She recalled Tim's parting comment. "I'm not going out with Tim," she rushed and then bit her lip, furious at herself for sounding so guilty. "I'm expecting Karyn to come over. We're going to talk over some plans for the basement." She grinned, her heart racing with anticipation. "Oh, Simon, you must come see the basement."

"What's new down there? More ghosts and goblins?"

"I don't think they're going to want to live there any more."

After placing the money safely in the cash register, she took his hand and hurried him through the store. The look on Simon's face when he saw the basement made every second of the tiresome and dirty job worthwhile. For a long while they sat side by side on the bottom step, talking about the basement and her aunt and the money. Noticeably absent in their rambling conversation was any mention of Simon's feelings about discovering her in Tim's embrace.

"Karyn will be here soon," Roseanna said, hoping her friend would hurry up and arrive. When Karyn came Simon would know she was telling the truth about her evening plans. "Why don't you stay and join us?" Linking arms, she leaned against him. "I'd love to have your input."

"Just what are you cooking up?"

She grinned. "Remember the afternoon we played records, and you came up with the idea of selling vintage clothing? Ever since that day the notion has been bouncing around in my imagination."

"You mean you're really going to do it?"

"That's what I had in mind."

"Hey, that's great." He squeezed her close. "I don't think I'll keep you girls company tonight, though. You two will probably talk clothes for hours. That would be hard to handle."

If he hadn't believed her, Roseanna though happily, he would have wanted to stay to see if Karyn really did turn up. She felt like pinching herself for allowing her old fears to torment her again. Simon trusted her.

After Simon departed Roseanna puttered around the store for another hour waiting for Karyn. Her friend was late, and when after another half hour she still hadn't arrived, Roseanna finally decided to head upstairs for the night.

Through her window, she saw lights on in Simon's back workroom. Had he been watching for Karyn's distinctive pink Jeep?

In a little while she heard knocking and went down to open the door. There was Karyn, looking as perky as ever in a miniscule polka-dot dress.

"Where have you been?" Roseanna exclaimed. "You're so late. I've been worried."

"Sorry. My car broke down and . . . oh, it's a long story. I got a ride from a neighbor." She grinned wickedly. "He's a doll, too. I almost abandoned you for him tonight."

It didn't take long in her high-spirited friend's company before Roseanna was relaxed and chattering nonstop. They were both starved so Roseanna fixed them glasses of wine and a plate of cheese and crackers. Sitting toe to toe with Karyn on the couch, with the big floor fan running on full speed, Roseanna told first about the money and then of her plans for the basement.

"Are you interested in helping?"

"Oh, Roseanna." Karyn gasped. "I would love to set up a vintage clothing boutique."

"It would be a small area at first to see how it goes over," Roseanna explained. "Of course I'd insist on paying you for your assistance."

Karyn shook her head, causing her cap of shiny dark hair to swing merrily. "Are you kidding? No way. It would be a blast."

Karyn wanted to start right away, and the very next evening they began. Simon was there, too, every night, building racks and dressing rooms while Karyn and Roseanna arranged the furnishings and painted the old mannequins bright colors. It was a lot of hard work, but being with Karyn and Simon made it fun.

By the following Sunday night, the basement was ready for the first clothing to be brought in.

Karyn put a finger to her poppy-red lips. "No, it's not done yet. It's very nice, but . . ."

"What?" asked Roseanna.

"I don't know . . ."

"What?" repeated Simon, in a sterner voice.

"I'm not sure. The final touch is missing," Karyn said, studying the freshly painted white walls. Karyn was in her element, bubbling over with enthusiasm. "Something unusual needs to be added, something to make it really special."

Roseanna shrugged. "Like?"

Karyn narrowed her eyes thoughtfully and then

broke out into a mysterious grin. "Roseanna, do you trust me?"

Roseanna and Simon looked at each other, brows raised.

"Of course," Roseanna said.

"Then let me have the basement to myself all day tomorrow. It's Monday. Since both shops are closed you two could have a day out or something. Just don't come back down here until I tell you to."

Roseanna decided that Karyn's suggestion to take the day off was an excellent one, especially since it prompted Simon to ask her to go sailing. By mid-morning they were on the water. Roseanna had fallen in love with his father's boat, the *Swallow,* and with sailing. She relaxed, content to let Simon show off his skill as he effortlessly guided the Concordia yawl through the deep blue water of the Chesapeake Bay. Roseanna wore only a bathing suit as she sat in the cockpit leaning against the varnished mahogany cabin side, and the sensation of wind against her sun-baked skin felt heavenly.

She observed Simon with open pleasure. He sat at the helm, his face into the wind, his expression an intriguing mix of exhilaration and serenity. With his ruggedly handsome features and long, strong limbs, he was the perfect complement to the classic wooden boat.

When they decided they were hungry, Roseanna fetched the picnic hamper Andrew had prepared for them and set out a meal of plump chicken sandwiches and tropical fruit salad. They ate in easy silence, look-ing at the beautiful homes tucked along the verdant shoreline and off in the distance three little white triangles, the sails of their companions on the water.

Simon handed her an iced coffee. "What on earth do you think Karyn is up to right now?"

"I have no clue." Roseanna stretched out her legs, loving the feel of the hot sun on them. "And today I don't even want to think about the store."

"No shop talk?"

Roseanna made a sudden decision. "Nope . . . except I do want to tell you one thing. I want to give that woman you recommended, Kate, a try."

"Good," was all Simon said. The warmth radiating from his eyes made her certain she was doing the right thing.

Roseanna could only finish half of her huge sandwich. Sipping her cold drink, she studied the wave pattern and thought about all the wonderful times she had shared with Simon. This day would stand out among the best of them.

"Do your sisters like to sail?" she asked conversationally.

"Madeline loves it, but Laura and Claire get seasick." He caught her eyes and gave her a meaningful look. "I think it's time you met everyone. The girls are spread out around the country, and it's a family tradition to gather at Dad's house for Thanksgiving. Will you come this year? I want to show you off."

Roseanna flushed with pleasure. "I'd love to. And I'd like you to meet my family, too."

"Who's the gorgeous one? Evelyn, right?" He gave her a broad teasing wink. "I'd really like to meet her."

Roseanna kicked at his thigh. "Don't get any ideas. Anyway, she's just gotten engaged."

"She's going to be Mrs. Politician?"

"Yep. She seems to have no more interest in modeling. Ever since she met Tom she's become more and more interested in politics. It's all she'll talk about these days. She says her dream of being a model was just a childhood fantasy, and that she is very glad now she didn't pursue it."

Simon captured her foot and began caressing it. "People have a way of growing and changing."

"Christie's changed, too. She said that my owning a business inspired her. Last month she opened a great daycare center in her house. Now she can stay home with her kids while she's bringing in an income. It's working out well. Although it isn't exactly the life she had dreamed of, she claims that in many ways it's so much better. She is very proud to be able to take care of her family so well."

"What about your brother?"

"He's planning on a long career in the Air Force. I think he genuinely loves it."

"What about you, Roseanna? Still holding on tight to your dream? Or have you changed, too?" His hands began to stroke her calf, and he looked at her with a sensual gleam in his eyes.

"How can I think about anything when you're doing that?" She reached into her glass and pulled out an ice cube to chuck at him. "Chill out."

He jumped up and snatched her wrist to pull her up beside him. "Come on, it's time you did some work around here." He placed her hands on the wooden wheel. "I'll show you how to steer." He pressed close to her and nuzzled her cheek. "Want to take it on your own?"

Smiling, Roseanna shook her head. "No. You need to stay here longer—a lot longer."

Roseanna felt wonderfully exhausted by the time she and Simon returned to Treasures that evening. They found Karyn, looking an adorable mess in paint-splattered overall shorts, slouched on the front porch drinking a soda.

"We just finished," she announced with great glee in her voice.

"Who's we?" Roseanna asked.

"Tim and I. He just took off. Left me with all the cleanup, the rat."

"Karyn, you're making me crazy! What has been going on here today?"

"Come and see." They followed her to the stairway, where she stopped and blocked their way. Her grin turned mischievous. "Wait. I have to turn out the lights."

Simon held Roseanna's hand as they descended into the darkness. Like her curiosity, the odor of oil paint and turpentine grew stronger with each step down-ward.

When they reached the bottom, Karyn shouted, "Okay, hit 'em!"

Roseanna felt around the wall for the switch, and the room flooded with light. She gasped. On one com-plete wall stretched a bold mural of a tropical island complete with palm trees, a treasure chest in the sand,

and pirates brandishing swords. In the arms of what looked to be the Lady Captain was a fierce black cat.

Roseanna began jumping in sheer delight before heading to the center of the room. She spun around, laughing. "Oh, my gosh! This is fantastic!"

Karyn grinned. "Tim did most of it. I just helped."

"I love it," Roseanna exclaimed. "It's perfect for the store."

"Imagine the basement filled with racks of super clothes," Karyn said. "A few pieces of funky furniture thrown in, like a purple dresser or some big, old gold mirrors . . . it's going to be fabulous!"

"It is. It truly is." Grabbing Karyn, Roseanna made her suffer an impulsive bear hug. "The customers will love it. Thank you so much."

"You're absolutely welcome." Karyn turned her around and propelled her back into Simon's arms, almost toppling her into a stack of paint cans.

"I think this effort deserves a pizza," Simon declared, and with Roseanna and Karyn's enthusiastic agreement, headed off to his favorite restaurant.

After he had departed Roseanna and Karyn cleaned the brushes with turpentine in the sink in the back, then took the smelly, damp rags and empty paint cans to add to the garbage heap.

Roseanna groaned. "I just remembered. I still have all that junk out back to haul away. I should have done it today." She recalled the sailing trip with Simon and felt her heart skip over itself. "I take that back. But it's got to go soon. It's been sitting in the alley for a week."

When they had finished and were waiting for Simon

to return Roseanna and Karyn sat on the basement steps talking over all their plans.

Karyn's expression became serious. "Roseanna, we need to talk." She sat leaning against the wall, her chin resting on her bent knees.

Roseanna looked up at her from her seat, two steps below. "What is it?"

"I know you don't like secondhand stuff. Ever since we met you've told me again and again about your plans to sell the store." Karyn drew a deep breath. "Well, I want to buy it."

"What?" Roseanna gaped at her friend in surprise.

"This last week, working here, building the clothing area, it's been so much fun. It's like a dream come true. It's what I've always wanted." She paused, as though gathering her thoughts. "Vintage clothes are my passion. I didn't realize how badly I wanted to make them my work until now."

Roseanna didn't know what to say. "B-but how would you pay for it?" she stammered.

"My grandmother's going to help me buy it. We'll be partners, with her taking over the upstairs while I focus on the downstairs. We were so excited that we drained three pots of coffee last night discussing it. Gram had adored being a businesswoman when she was younger, and had always wanted to have a store again. But time slipped by. Then, as we talked, it was as though she had a revelation that it's not too late to go after an old dream."

"This is so sudden," Roseanna said, her head reeling.

Karyn's face glowed. "It'll be a great combination,

the retro clothes, the antiques, and the funky second-hand."

If anyone were going to buy her store Roseanna would have wanted it to be Karyn. But even though selling the place had been her plan from the beginning, for some reason Roseanna didn't feel elated. In fact, she felt oddly numb instead. It felt as though a hole had opened in her heart and all the joy was pouring out.

"I'll have to think about it," she responded, keeping her voice neutral.

Karyn's brow puckered. She scrutinized Roseanna for a long moment before her expression changed to one of surprise and comprehension. "Why, Roseanna MacAuly. You're hesitating! I thought you'd leap at the chance to get out from under this place. What's happened?"

Roseanna lifted her shoulders. "I don't know. Isn't that strange? I really don't know."

Simon returned with a large box releasing delicious odors and they all went upstairs to eat, talking and laughing. Roseanna tried to put her conversation with Karyn aside, but it continued to buzz inside her head like an annoying bee. Did she want to sell or not?

When only two slices of Hawaiian pizza remained, Karyn pushed herself to her feet complaining she'd eaten too much, grabbed her backpack, and departed.

As soon as she had gone, the atmosphere became intimate. Simon looked so handsome with his skin browned from the brilliant summer sunshine and his thick hair tousled by the wind. Smiling softly, Rose-anna met his gaze, trying to tell him with her eyes how very deeply she cared for him. He pulled her into the circle of his arms.

"Have I told you lately how impressed I am with what you've done to this store?" he murmured, brushing wisps of hair from her cheek and tucking it behind her ear.

Flushing from his compliment, she beamed up at him. "Every time you see it."

"Well, I'm going to say it again. Darling, you amaze me. You have amazed me since the day I met you. And I have the feeling you will continue to amaze me for as long as I know you. And I hope that is a long, long time." He cupped her chin in the palm of his hand and smiled down at her. "I remember when you disliked this store and couldn't wait for the day you sold it. But you know what? I think that's all changed. I think you've become very attached to this old place."

"I-I suppose I have," Roseanna agreed, her emotions more tangled than ever. "Simon, I have to tell you something. Just now, while you were gone, Karyn told me she wanted to buy the store. She and her grandmother together." She filled him in on the details. "I'm kind of in shock."

His face altered before her eyes, all the joy draining away. He frowned down at her, his expression more somber than she had seen in a long time. After a few silent moments, he asked, "Have you made a decision?"

"I haven't had time to think about it," she replied in a subdued voice. "Karyn will be getting her dream store, and I will be free to create mine."

"The clothing boutique."

"Yes. What I've always wanted."

As though he sensed her shaky emotions and how much she needed to be comforted, he opened his arms to invite her inside for a hug. She leaned against him, savoring his masculine strength. Tucked inside his arms, life seemed easy.

"Be careful," he whispered into her hair. "Take your time to decide. You love this place more than you realize."

Chapter Ten

Roseanna was dancing. Somewhere in the back-
ground came the sound of a drum, faint at first, then
becoming louder and louder. She danced on. Someone
was calling her name, calling her name. . . .

She woke up with a start.

The thumping noise continued. She sat up in bed
and rubbed her eyes, trying to understand what the
sound was and where it was coming from. As the fog
of sleep cleared she realized someone was pounding
on her downstairs door.

The room was dark. She turned on her nightstand
light and checked her alarm clock. It was just after
midnight. Throwing on her bathrobe, she raced to the
window to see if Simon's back lights were on. When
she saw that they were, she felt a wave of relief. He
was over there working. Maybe he had needed to talk

to her about something and thought she was up. Maybe he had hurt himself on a power tool and needed her help right away. The thumping went on, sounding more and more urgent. She ran down the stairs and unlocked the door. Before she could properly open it, Tim was pushing inside.

His face was ashen and his eyes wild.

"Tim! What's going on!" she gasped.

He grabbed her arm. "I need to use your phone," he shouted, pushing her aside and bounding up the stairs.

Roseanna raced after him. Tim was already punching out a number when she joined him. "I'm calling to report a fire," he yelled into the receiver. He gave them the address. "Yes, we're leaving the building now. There's no one else inside."

Fire. The building was on fire? She gaped at him, uncomprehending, but Tim's grim expression told her it was all too true. Panic set in at once, and she looked around her as if in a drunken daze, confused as to what to do next.

Tim dropped the phone, and it went clanging onto the floor. "Come on. We're getting out of here."

"I—I need my slippers," she insisted. "And . . . and, oh, my necklace!"

"Don't be stupid," he exclaimed, grabbing her arm.

But the idea spun in her whirling mind. It was all she could think of. She must have the necklace.

Yanking loose of his grip, she dashed headlong for the bedroom. Her heartbeat hammered in her ears, drowning out his shouts. Where were the slippers? Her gaze swept around the room and then landed, not on the shoes but on her jewelry box. The necklace. She must have the necklace!

Snatching the box, she dumped it upside down on her comforter, found the jewelry, and stuffed it into her bathrobe pocket. Twirling around, her hand hit her water glass and sent it crashing to the floor. She dove beneath the bed for her slippers.

That's when she saw Captain Blackbeard. How could she have forgotten him? He crouched there, just out of reach.

"Captain," she coaxed. "Come—"

She didn't have a chance to say more. Strong hands gripped her around the waist and were hauling her backward.

"Roseanna, we have to go!" Fear and anger contorted Tim's voice. "Forget the cat."

"No," she screamed at him, trying to twist and tug out of his grasp. Her bare foot landed on the shattered glass, and she cried out when she felt it cut. Then she smelled smoke and forgot the pain. The building was really burning. "I'm not leaving him—"

"Come on!" he cut her off. Ignoring her frantic protests, he dragged her out of the room and down the hall. By the time they got to the stairway, tears streamed down her face, and Tim's shirt had been ripped open from her struggles. She fought him every step of the way down and out into the courtyard.

There, the loud wail of sirens broke the runaway train of her panic, and she stopped flailing. Tears welled up and overflowed down her cheeks. "Tim, please," she implored, her voice barely making it past the sobs.

"Don't worry. The firemen will get the cat," he assured her in a gentle, worried voice. Then he looked down and saw the pool of blood around her foot. "Oh, no—you're hurt!" He swept her into his arms.

Through bleary eyes she saw the fire engines coming up the street. Simon ran toward them.

"Simon," she cried out as he approached. "The building is on fire. Captain is still upstairs!"

Simon halted, his assessing gaze raking the two of them. "Where is he?"

"Under the bed," Tim answered.

Without another word, he ran for the stairs. Roseanna could see smoke rising from behind the building. Then, as if by magic, noise and commotion erupted around them as the street filled with fire trucks and police cars. The fire chief jogged over to them.

"Anyone inside?"

"Yes," she gasped. "Simon Oakes. He just went upstairs after my cat."

The fire chief poured rapid-fire instructions into his walkie-talkie, and then Roseanna saw two firemen dash toward the stairway. Moments later the firemen and Simon emerged and headed toward them. To her infinite relief she saw a struggling black mass in Simon's arms.

"You live here, Miss?" the fire chief asked.

"Yes. And I have the business downstairs."

The walkie-talkie crackled and Roseanna could here someone speaking. "Front door's not locked. We're going in."

"Not locked?" The fire chief turned his surprised gaze to her.

Roseanna shook her head, confused. "I don't know. I was sure I locked the place."

The fire chief departed just as Simon walked up holding Captain tight against his chest. Tim shifted her in his arms. It took the sight of Simon's frosty glare and rock-hard jaw to make her realize how things must look to Simon. A kind of desperation pulsed through her veins, and she strained against his grip.

"Put me down, Tim," she demanded, and reluctantly he set her on her one good foot. She wobbled, and he wrapped an arm around her waist to steady her. "Tim rescued me," she explained.

"I was passing by and saw smoke," Tim rushed, acting as flustered as a teenager. He looked worriedly at Roseanna. "Right?"

"What a coincidence," muttered Simon. His dark eyes bore into hers like silent accusers.

Her face feeling like it was burning too, Roseanna tore her gaze away and clutched her bathrobe tightly to her. Seeing Tim's open shirt, disheveled hair, and red face, she realized that Tim's explanation had sounded questionable to Simon. It looked as though they had been together when the fire started.

Simon's expression clearly revealed his thoughts. He suspected she was lying. He thought she and Tim were romantically involved! His wife had cheated on him, and now he believed Roseanna had, too. He didn't trust her after all. Had he *ever* trusted her? She whirled away from him, feeling a pain in her heart unlike anything she had experienced before.

All around them the world had turned upside-down. Sirens blasted her ears and the acrid smell of smoke tore at her nostrils. She saw no flames, but knew Treasures was on fire somewhere she could not yet see. Firemen hurried past her, intent on their tasks.

Tim squeezed her close. "You okay?"

"I'm fine now. You can go," she told him. "Thanks."

Tim flicked a glance from her angry face to Simon's. "You sure?" He seemed at a loss for what else to say, and when Roseanna nodded he shrugged. "Call me."

After Tim had departed, she and Simon stood together in subzero silence. She stepped down on her cut foot and winced.

"You're hurt."

She shook her head. "It's just a scratch."

"Come over to my place, and let me look at it," he demanded.

"No. The first-aid truck is just over there. They'll fix me up." She kept her eyes trained on the building. "I don't want to leave until I know what's happening here. You go on. Take Captain away from here before he scratches you to pieces."

"Not until I see that you're taken care of."

He escorted her to the aid truck and waited outside while she was being helped. The cut was small for how much it had bled, and it didn't take long to be cleaned and bandaged.

With Captain contained under one strong arm, Simon assisted her out of the back of the truck. Before he had a chance to say anything the fire chief arrived.

"You were lucky, Miss," the burly man informed her, wiping sweat from his brow. "If the smoke had been spotted much later things could have been a lot worse. Most of the damage is confined to a small area of the back wall."

"Oh, thank heaven," Roseanna exclaimed in relief. "Do you know what caused it?"

The fire chief wedged his hands on his hips and looked down at her from his considerable height. "Yep. We have an idea, all right. Looks like a pile of trash got left out back of this old firetrap. Lots of flammable stuff like stacks of newspaper, cardboard boxes full of clothes, and old wood furniture that was dry as tinder."

Roseanna frowned, confused. "But what started the fire?"

"The evidence points to spontaneous combustion. We saw some oil paint cans, solvents, and rags."

The fire chief fixed Roseanna with a pointed stare. "Have you been painting recently?"

"Yes," she answered, her voice thin from the misery seeping into her soul.

"Probably solvent on those rags, and that's what did it," the fire chief concluded.

When the big man departed, Simon turned to Roseanna. "You're not going to be able to go back into this building tonight. Stay with me."

It was more an order than an invitation. At his hostile tone, a thick wall began erecting around her heart. Roseanna knew exactly what was going on with Simon, and she just didn't possess the emotional strength to deal with his jealousy tonight.

"No, thanks anyway. I have a place to stay." She

would be welcomed at home or at her sister's or Karyn's, of course.

"With Tim?"

"What do you care?" She knew he would come to his own conclusions no matter what she said. When she had the sudden desire to slap his stonelike face, she knew she needed to get away from him. "I'm feeling a little shaky," she told him tersely. "I'm going to sit in the aid truck for a few minutes."

"Why won't you come home with me?" he demanded.

She gave him a frosty look. "I think you know the answer to that." She turned to leave.

He reached out and caught her arm, halting her in her tracks. "Roseanna, just answer this. What was Tim doing in your apartment?"

"You know what," she hissed, jerking her arm free. "Rescuing me."

Simon's mouth took an ugly sarcastic twist. "It sure was lucky he happened to be passing by."

Frustration sent a flood of tears spewing forth. "I should have known better than to take a chance on a secondhand man," she sputtered.

"And I should have known better than to trust again."

The last she saw of Simon was his rigid back as he headed away from her.

"Roseanna, are you up?" Karyn called out. "I'm done in the bathroom."

For a week Roseanna had camped out on Karyn's living-room futon. She had placed a sign on Treasures' doors to let her customers know the store would be closed temporarily because of fire damage, and then had not gone back. She did not have the emotional energy to deal with the store yet.

Roseanna pushed herself off the bed, sending her lightweight blanket to the floor. It had been another sleepless night, and she felt groggy. She pulled on shorts and a top, and then went out to sit at the bistro table on Karyn's second-floor balcony.

The apartment overlooked a serene grassy field bordered by a grove of birch trees. Sunlight bathed the area, drying the dew and filling the air with the smell of late summer. She heard barking and saw the energetic Jack Russell from a neighbor's apartment chasing squirrels. The dog's elderly owner called out a cheerful good morning to her. The sound of humming came from the kitchen where Karyn was no doubt making the tea she could not start the day without. Life was going on without Roseanna.

"Breakfast is ready," Karyn announced in her sunny voice, bringing a tray outside loaded with bright orange melon wedges and warm croissants. She wore a vintage summer shift of daffodil yellow, and her eyes sparkled with vitality even at this early hour.

Captain Blackbeard joined them, wandering about the porch testing the air. When he saw the dog he arched his back fiercely, making Roseanna smile. She had been so glad to see Blackbeard again when Karyn had brought him over from Simon's.

"How are you feeling this morning?" Karyn asked as she poured a cup of Earl Grey for Roseanna.

"Restless."

"Moping around here isn't helping, is it?"

"If I go back to my place Simon might show up." Just the thought of that happening caused her heart to constrict painfully.

"It wouldn't hurt just to talk to him," Karyn advised. "Aren't you ever going to speak to him?"

Roseanna focused on the cream and sugar she was stirring into her tea. "A clean break is hard enough. What's the point of seeing him again? It would only make me feel even more miserable."

"Talk to him, Roseanna! He was caught by surprise that night, and he jumped to conclusions. He will believe you didn't have Tim in your apartment that night," Karyn insisted, her tone now taking on an edge of exasperation. "Tell him the police found Tim's jacket inside the store, and it will clear up everything."

"You know, Simon seemed to sense something amiss with Tim all along. I always assumed he was just jealous."

"He might have been a little bit. It's only natural, Roseanna. Especially since it was obvious Tim had a thing for you."

When Tim's coat had been discovered on the floor inside the unlocked store, the mystery of the nighttime noises was solved. The odd little sounds had not been made by mice but by Tim, who had made a key for himself and had been letting himself in to search for treasure hidden by her aunt.

Of course Roseanna had had to tell Tim she no longer wanted him to work at the shop, but refused to go so far as to prosecute. It appeared he had done no harm other than cause worrisome noises, and she owed him a great debt for rescuing her and saving the store when he could have simply fled.

Roseanna shook her head stubbornly. "I refuse to tell him about Tim. Don't you see? It would be as though I had to prove my innocence. I will not have a man in my life who doesn't completely trust me."

"It was just one stupid moment. Can't you forgive him that?"

"It was a very revealing moment."

Karyn set her cup sharply in its saucer. "Roseanna, when are you going to understand that Simon loves you. And he does trust you, I know he does. What happened with your jerk of an ex-boyfriend, Gary, isn't happening again. Gary and Simon are different men."

"Different men, same circumstance." The image of Simon's ice-cold eyes when he found her and Tim together the night of the fire haunted her. He had automatically assumed she was guilty. And no explanations would have appeased him.

Although she hated what Simon had done to her, the pain of letting him go was nearly more than she could bear. She clutched her cup tightly, trying to keep her fingers from trembling. "When you don't learn from your mistakes," she intoned bitterly, "life has a curious way of repeating itself."

A thoughtful silence descended over the porch while they finished their tea. Then, with a determined look on her face, Karyn rose to her feet. "Roseanna, come with me."

"Huh?"

"It's time for you to go home."

"Oh, Karyn. I'm sorry. I didn't realize I'd overstayed my welcome." Roseanna trailed behind her friend, feeling worse than ever.

Karyn dug Roseanna's suitcase out of her overflowing closet and tossed it on the bed. Racks filled with the retro clothing Karyn wanted to sell made the room feel cramped and crowded.

"Don't be ridiculous. I love having you here." Karyn's mouth opened and then closed, as though she considered saying more but then changed her mind. "Listen to me. You just need to go. You can't hide out here wallowing in self-pity forever."

"I think having a broken heart justifies taking some time to feel rotten," Roseanna returned sourly, stuffing clothes into her bag.

"Time's up," Karyn returned. "Your customers want you back."

"I suppose I should attend to Treasures," Roseanna grumbled. She looked hard at Karyn. There was an easy way out of this whole mess. A way where she could leave and never see Simon again. "Is your offer to buy the store still good?"

"Not for a while, it's not."

"What do you mean?"

"You're upset right now. I won't let you make that kind of decision while you're in this frame of mind." Karyn came over and placed a hand on Roseanna's shoulder. "Let's leave it up in the air for a bit, okay?"

Roseanna shrugged.

"Ready to go?" Karyn asked, heading out the door.

"Almost." She placed Captain Blackbeard in the pet carrier. "All right. I'm set. Let's go."

Now that she had said it she found she was eager to return to the secondhand store. She missed being there. She missed her customers. Keeping herself cooped up in Karyn's apartment had only made her more depressed. Perhaps if she stayed busy life would become tolerable without Simon.

Karyn gave her an encouraging smile. "I'll drop you off on my way to work."

It was a typical Maryland September morning, hot, sunny, and humid. Karyn rolled up the canvas sides of her pink jeep and tossed Roseanna's suitcase into the back. Roseanna placed the cat carrier at her feet. They started off, the breeze that tossed her hair about wonderfully reviving.

"You *were* right," Roseanna admitted, talking loudly over the rush of air and road sounds. "I'm feeling better already."

Karyn passed a newly constructed strip mall. A lot of those spaces were still for lease, and it would be a great location for a clothing boutique. Still, Roseanna didn't like the place, and was at a loss to explain her lack of enthusiasm. Six months ago the site would have sent a surge of excitement through her. Now the sprawling concrete-and-glass structure seemed dreadfully dull.

The mall owner would have all kinds of codes and restrictions, she suspected. It was doubtful he would allow the kind of abandoned creativity that she enjoyed now. Inevitably her boutique would end up a clone of every other one in the area. Suddenly, the thought of leaving Treasures made her terribly sad.

Roseanna realized how infrequently she thought

about her old dream. Building up Treasures had been such an all-consuming—and even fun—challenge that she had forgotten about her ultimate goal.

"You've made that secondhand store unique and people adore it," Karyn said, seeming to read Roseanna's mind. "Who needs another boring clothing boutique?"

Had the idea been just a young girl's fantasy? Roseanna wondered. She thought about her sisters and brother, how their childhood fantasies had changed or evolved into different, even more wonderful dreams. Instead of pining over lost desires, they were actively engaged in creating new lives for themselves.

The secondhand store Roseanna had never wanted felt like a part of her. The sweat and tears and love she'd poured into turning Treasures into a money-maker had forged a bond. She had fallen in love with Treasures, she realized, just as she had with Simon, resisting every inch of the way.

Maybe it was time to let the childhood dream go and keep the secondhand store. The notion startled her, causing her to sit up straight, thinking hard. Keep Treasures? Let the old dream go? Why not? It seemed so right, so wonderfully right. She took a deep breath, sighing with relief.

An idea occurred to her. "Karyn, I know what to do," she blurted out. "I won't sell the store to you. What I will do is sublease the basement to you and your grandmother. I don't have a real interest in vintage clothing like you do, so it would be fine with me not to take that on. We can all work together in the same building and can help each other out."

Karyn whooped, her face splitting into a huge grin. "Oh, Roseanna, that's perfect. You're on, girl." She stuck her arm toward Roseanna at an awkward angle to seal the agreement with a handshake.

As they neared the store Roseanna perked up, surprised to see an unusual amount of traffic near her parking lot.

"Hey," she gasped, staring at the merchandise filling the courtyard. A large hand-lettered sign by the side of the road announced a fire sale.

"What's going on?" Roseanna looked around in stunned disbelief as Karyn whipped into the busy parking area. "How—"

"Surprise," Karyn said, her huge smile still plastered across her face. "Sorry I can't stay. I've got to work. But I'm giving notice this morning."

Roseanna climbed out of the Jeep, her head spinning. "Who did all this?"

"Simon and his dad and I," Karyn told her, her gaze connecting with Roseanna's in a meaningful way. "It was Simon who convinced the landlord it would be in his best interest to get repairs done, pronto."

"Why did Simon do this?"

Karyn rolled her eyes. "You figure it out."

"Probably some misguided sense of responsibility," she concluded on an irritable note as she hauled out her suitcase and the cat carrier.

Roseanna eyed her suspiciously. "Did you tell him about Tim?"

She raised her hands. "No way. I don't butt into other people's business."

When Karyn headed out, Roseanna wove her way

through the crowd in the courtyard. She spotted Simon at once, and as though he sensed her presence, he turned just then to impale her with his questioning gaze. The impact from the eye contact halted her in her tracks and sent her heart catapulting into her throat.

He made his way toward her, his expression wary. "Hello, Roseanna," he said, the soft timbre of his voice washing over her like a warm wave.

Roseanna could not seem to manage any more coherent thoughts. "I—I don't know what to say. Thank you, I guess."

Silence hung between them. She supposed he was waiting for her to let him know how she felt. Oh, how she wanted just to melt into his arms and forget everything except her love for him. But her uncertainty paralyzed her.

His gaze devouring her, he reached out slowly to brush a stray hair from her cheek. Her lips parted, but she could force out no words. Tears began to burn the back of her eyes and she looked away.

"Now that you're here," he finally said, "I guess I'll head out and let you get on with it."

Dazed, she watched him jog across the street and disappear into his own shop. She went inside her own store, where she released Captain and then went at once to check out the damage to the building. There was a faint lingering odor of smoke, and a ten-foot square patch of new siding on the back wall, but that was all. Her heart swelling in gratitude, she whispered a thank you to Simon.

Returning to the desk, she sat down to try to gather

her thoughts. Only a moment had passed before a tall, thin man came inside holding a brass lamp he wanted to purchase. A plump young woman with two identical dark-eyed little girls each hugging sock monkeys lined up behind the man. Another customer called out for assistance. He wanted the stuffed marlin. After that there was no time to dwell on anything but business.

By 5:00 Roseanna was exhausted. Taking an iced tea with her, she went outside to sit on the front steps to cool down as best she could in the sultry evening. She still had a courtyard full of merchandise to bring in, but it could wait a few minutes.

After the hectic hours before, the evening seemed unusually quiet and peaceful and . . . lonely. She rested her elbows on her knees and cupped her chin in her palms, her mind going over the events of the day. Wouldn't Simon be pleased when she told him how well the sale had gone? But when would she tell him? He wouldn't be coming over almost daily to check on her the way he had done before. The way things stood, he would surely avoid her.

The thought of never seeing him again caused a terrible ache to radiate from the center of her being. It was a torment to continue dwelling on him, but she could not seem to push him from her mind.

She recalled their volatile first encounter. What an impression he had made! His arrogant self-confidence and virile masculinity had nearly overwhelmed her. His powerful personality could still intimidate her sometimes, but now she knew he also possessed so many other characteristics. Tenderness. Joyfulness. Passion. She admired so much about him.

Stinging tears welled and she brushed them away with the back of her hand. Misery made her limbs heavy, making it an effort to push herself up and go inside. How she would miss him. She thought of the many hours they had spent together, how they had gotten to know each other and grown close. She knew he was responsible for the way she now felt about Treasures.

He had cleaned up after the fire, had the building repaired, and arranged this sale. He had done it all for her. But he hadn't called her. What did that mean?

Her heart provided the answer. He loved her, that was what. He might be scared, like she was, and stubborn, like she was, but just as Karyn told her, Simon's love glowed in his eyes. She had felt it in his kisses. He loved her, and he was not going to let her go. And heaven help her, she did not want him to.

He was secondhand; she could not change that. But suddenly it did not matter anymore. She had been terribly wrong and terribly foolish to let past wounds govern her heart, for her fears might have cost her the love of a lifetime.

That realization brought a rush of relief and then a surge of joyous excitement. Roseanna knew what to do now. She would go to him tonight—no, right now, and tell him what was in her heart.

Nearly shaking with fear and excitement, Roseanna headed inside to phone him. When she reached her desk she noticed the empty cat carrier and realized she had not seen Captain for a while. He was always so good about staying in the store that she never worried much about him. But so many people were in and out today, he might have slipped out when someone went through the door.

"Blacky," she called. The store seemed so quiet after all the hubbub of the day. She called again, hurried to the rear, and called a third time. She looked in all his favorite hiding places, but it was as though he had vanished. Prickles of worry raced up her spine.

She was peering under a table when the sound of human footsteps made her jump. Then the small hairs at the back of her neck rose and her breath came in shallow gulps. She dared not hope. She slowly turned around to see Simon striding toward her, holding the black feline in his arms.

"I had a visitor this evening," he told her as he approached. He stopped a few feet from her and set the cat down. "I thought you might be wondering what happened to him."

"Oh, I was so scared." She bent to stroke the cat and when she rose somehow Simon had moved to mere inches from her. It was impossible to catch her breath. She couldn't keep her feelings for him inside one second longer. "I was so scared. . . ." She faltered, and then regained her courage. "I was so afraid I had lost you, Simon."

A tear spilled over, making a hot trail down her cheek. He reached over to gently wipe it away.

"I know. The last week has been a nightmare for me, too." He puffed out a breath and his expression turned to one of painful remorse. "I acted like an idiot the night of the fire. When I saw you and Tim together, it looked so bad that my old fears jumped out and took a strangle hold on me. I was so jealous I lost control of my common sense."

Recalling the awful scene, Roseanna grimaced. "And your behavior was proof I had been right all along, that you couldn't be trusted to believe in me."

He shook his head, his anger toward himself clearly apparent. "It took a while to cool down, but I finally realized how wrong I had been. I was terrified that I had driven you away."

"Why didn't you come to me?"

He ran a hand through his hair. "You needed some time to think things through. I acted like a fool, and I was hoping you'd forgive me. I didn't want to pressure you."

"Did you know about Tim being in the store that night?" His mystified expression assured her he was still in the dark, so she quickly told the story.

As her emotions raged out of control she cried brokenly, "Oh, Simon. I don't just care for you. I've fallen in love with you. I know I shouldn't have, but there it is."

"And why shouldn't you have?" His voice sounded steady and sure, while she felt about to shatter into a million pieces.

He gripped her waist, drawing her close until she melted into his strong embrace. "Oh, Roseanna," he murmured into her hair. "I think I began to love you the first day I saw you here."

"You love me, too?" She wanted to hear him say if over and over.

Instead, his mouth claimed hers, telling her so much more than he could with any words. She responded to his kiss with wholehearted joy. They finally broke apart, breathing hard. She lay her head against his shoulder, reveling in the feel of him, and thought about all that had happened.

"Simon, I came so close to selling the shop to Karyn," she told him, still in a daze. "I didn't know until this morning that I couldn't. I've grown so fond of this old place, the funky stuff, the fun of finding antiques. I really like them."

"I can hardly believe I am hearing you say that," Simon murmured, backing away so he could look into her eyes.

"It's all because of you, you know." She smiled all of her love at him. "Your enthusiasm was contagious. Your excitement made me excited. A year ago if you had told me I would feel this way, I would have keeled over in laughter. Now I'm proud of this store, as proud as I ever would have been of a clothing boutique. While staying at Karyn's I missed the store badly, and I missed my apartment. It feels like home."

He leaned over to whisper a kiss across her mouth. "I hope you won't be too upset leaving it."

"What do you mean?"

He shrugged, the devilish gleam she adored once more dancing in his amber eyes. "Well, after we get married, I'll expect you to live with me. We'll buy a house."

Roseanna stared at him, stunned. "Married? You and me?"

"Those are the two people I had in mind." He chuckled, fishing into his pocket. "I have something for you." He drew out a blue velvet box and opened it to reveal a stunning diamond ring. "It's secondhand, I'm afraid."

"Oh, Simon, I don't care about that anymore."

The twinkle in his eyes told her he was teasing. "It belonged to my mother."

"That makes it even more wonderful." Roseanna's hand was shaking when she held it out for Simon to slip on the engagement ring. "Oh, Simon. It's incredibly beautiful."

"Does this mean you accept?"

She was laughing and crying and nodding all at once. "I used to think you were a secondhand man."

"What am I now?"

She smiled and kissed him. "My treasure."